Daddy's Boy

CONNIE NORMAN

Publishing Partners
2024

Publishing Partners
Port Townsend, WA
marcia@marciabreece.com
www.marciabreece.com

Copyright © 2024 Connie V. Norman

All rights reserved. No part of this book may be reproduced, stored in, or introduced into a retrieval system, or transmitted in any form, or by any means (electronic, mechanical, photocopying, recording, or otherwise) without the prior written permission of the publisher.

ISBN: 978-1-944887-89-6

Contents

Chapter 1 1
Chapter 2 7
Chapter 3 14
Chapter 4 21
Chapter 5 26
Chapter 6 29
Chapter 7 36
Chapter 8 40
Chapter 9 43
Chapter 10 47
Chapter 11 50
Chapter 12 58
Chapter 13 69
Chapter 14 74
Chapter 15 80
Chapter 16 85
Chapter 17 92
Chapter 18 95
Chapter 19 99
Chapter 20 107
Chapter 21 113
Chapter 22 117
Chapter 23 123
Chapter 24 126
Chapter 25 134
Chapter 26 138
Chapter 27 144
Chapter 28 151
Chapter 29 156
Chapter 30 160
Chapter 31 165
Chapter 32 172
Chapter 34 177
Chapter 34 187
Chapter 35 191
Chapter 36 195
Chapter 37 197
Chapter 38 202
Chapter 39 207

CHAPTER 1

Jeff stood in front of the bathroom mirror checking his refection as he put the finishing touches on his black necktie. "Why did I let Kevin talk me into going to this stupid banquet? God, I hate parties," he muttered to Duffy, his wheaten colored cairn terrier. "Everybody standing around trying to make small talk. If only people would just stop feeling sorry for me. One more fix up or planned chance meeting at someone's backyard barbecue and I'll go into hiding for the rest of my natural life." But Jeff had no portent that this one, single night would launch a chain of events that would alter the course of his life.

It was a formal dinner given by Kevin's boss, an annual summer event; however, this year, instead of the Bonaventure Hotel, the dinner was to be held at one of the most prestigious (and pricey) country clubs in the Los Angeles area. It was only Kevin's big "sell job" of the place that finally convinced Jeff to attend. He had secretly held a vivid curiosity about this swanky private club.

"Come on, man," Kevin had pleaded. "I'm not doin' this for you. I'm asking you to do it for me. There's gonna be a sit down dinner, a live band and tons of single women. I need an ally."

Kevin Swensen worked for McCormick, a large pharmaceutical company, as an outside salesman so he rarely got a chance to meet any of the other employees. The company employed over five hundred people but the only one Kevin knew well was his secretary, Jane, who was in her fifties, married and a grandmother of five.

A blond, tan, California boy type of twenty-eight, Kevin took every opportunity that came along to gather as many new love interests as was humanly possible. Jeff, on the other hand, was quite a bit more reserved even though he was considered by many to be the more handsome of the two. They had met on a golf course six years earlier and had become the most unlikely of best friends—Kevin outgoing, flirtatious—Jeff introspective, intellectual.

He ran the nylon comb through his thick, dark hair then walked over to the full-length mirror for one last glance at his overall appearance. A tall, well-built man with quiet, chestnut eyes gazed back at him. It was a face that emitted a lost expression—a forlorn face, all of thirty years of age.

He had tried not to allow himself to think about it, but thoughts of Amber flooded his mind. A five-year relationship over for the past four months. She had sat him down one night at the kitchen table and announced that she was going to have to move on. Their early relationship agreement had been "no kids." But Amber claimed to have changed her mind in the past year. Said that her time clock was ticking and she could not afford to waste any time on a relationship that wasn't headed in that direction. Not only had she decided that she wanted to become a mother all of a sudden, but she became obsessed with having a baby—a fixation that had grown to consume her every waking thought.

Being the oldest child in a chaotic family with eleven brothers and sisters, Jeff now had zero desire to become a parent. His entire childhood was taken up with babysitting, changing diapers, cleaning up messes and never having one tiny nuance of privacy. Solitude was always that elusive butterfly.

Since both his mother and father worked long hours at menial jobs to make ends meet, he was expected to come straight home from school to help with grocery shopping, dinner and getting the kids bathed and ready for bed. The job of seeing to it that the school aged kids completed their homework each night also fell onto his worn-out shoulders. His weekends, as well, were filled with chores around the house; laundry, yard work, housework and handling various emergencies that would never cease to emerge with all of those kids tearing through the house and getting into things that would boggle the imagination. No sooner would he tend to one crisis than another would erupt in a different part of the house.

Jeff resented his parents bitterly for burdening him with what he thought should have been their job. He certainly did not ask for such a miserable childhood. Any kinds of sports, hobbies or even close friendships were out of the question. Being forced to stay up until all hours to get his required studying and homework done, he vividly remembered being always overwhelmed—in a continuous state of exhaustion. And worst of all, he lived his whole life in one desperate effort to tune out the ear-splitting racket of all those brats incessantly running in and out of the house. It was twenty-four-hour pandemonium.

When Amber dropped this bombshell on him, he tried with every ounce of his being to come to terms with the idea. But each time he thought it through; he landed unequivocally in the same damn place. No kids! He loved her but if her mind was so locked on having rug rats, he had no choice but to wish her well in her search for the right man to sire her offspring. His parenting days were over…period!

And besides, two years into their relationship, they had had a scare thinking that Amber might be pregnant. Jeff immediately flipped into panic mode and started at the top of the list of urologists in the yellow pages. After repeatedly hearing the same crap that the doctor's first opening is six goddamned months from now, he finally ended his hysterical search in the middle of the "N" section—receiving a next week appointment with a Doctor H. Nouvouyan. He closed his eyes and prayed that this did not mean he was placing his precious jewels in the hands of some quack. Why wasn't this guy booked into the next century like all the others?

A trembling Jeffrey placed his bare feet into the cold, metal stirrups of Doctor Nouvouyan's narrow operating table. He quickly became aware of the reason it was so easy to get in to see this doctor—he had no people skills whatsoever! He spoke English well enough. That wasn't the problem. It was his personality—or lack thereof. Every time Jeff started to ask a question, his hand would go up in a "stick a cork in it" gesture. And his nurse was his wife—a dark, no expression woman with the charisma of wallpaper paste—a perfect pair, the two of them.

The doc gave him a Valium fifteen minutes before he came in with the instruments of torture (or permanent disfigurement, or worse). This and a teeny injection at the sight were supposed to be plenty of anesthesias for a simple, non-invasive surgery.

"I don't know how in the hell I'm lying there when he comes at me with this dagger," he spouts off to Kevin afterwards. "I try to tell Numb Nuts that my nuts aren't numb yet, but every time I start to say, 'Doc, I can still feel…,' up goes the hand!"

With the soreness he had to endure after the "procedure," he was convinced that he had run off half cocked to "Doctor Sensitivity," but in time the tenderness subsided and the old machinery was back in full operation. In fact, sex was better than ever now that he had been relieved of the ever-looming terror of pregnancy.

When Amber's period finally came, there was a whopping sigh of relief on Jeff's part and what looked, now that he thought about it, like a ting of disappointment in Amber's eyes. Now, in order to go along with her new life direction, he would have to have his vasectomy reversed and he was sure as hell not going through anything like that again!

Still, his heart was smarting from this recent turn of events. He and Amber had planned to marry and grow old together… just the two of them. Nice and quiet. Take long vacations…see the world…play golf on Saturdays…sleep late and read the paper in bed with a cup of coffee on Sunday mornings. His life would have been perfect; all planned out and tucked in real comfy. Now this!

He called Amber from time to time just to see how things were going for her. Maybe she would miss the shit out of him and return to her senses. But no such luck. In fact, she had already become involved with some dipshit she claimed to have met on an Internet dating service. Jeff thought maybe he was being played for a chump for the last months of their relationship.

Jeff's friends and co-workers immediately became locked on an indefatigable quest to get him "hooked up." They would dredge up dates for him from God only knew where. But, he wasn't ready and each attempt at matchmaking turned out to be a huge catastrophe in one way or another.

One girl got dead drunk on their dinner date and passed out cold in his car on the way back to her apartment. He had no choice but to carry her up the stairs while she proceeded to vomit her lobster and creamed spinach all over his Armani suit.

Another one that stood out was a "set up" from a cousin of a brother of a friend of a friend—a skinny redhead (what the hell was her name?) whose boyfriend had apparently followed them on their dinner and movie date. Bad enough that she had displayed a tattoo of a striking cobra on her shoulder blade and spent the entire evening smacking on gum, but after the show let out and they walked up to Jeff's car in the parking lot, there was a biker dude leaning against the passenger side door. "Would you mind not leaning on my car?" he addressed the stranger.

"Fuck you, shithead." This led to a shouting match between the two men during which Jeff was crudely informed that his date was the girlfriend of this tattoo laden, leather bound thug. But the acrimony came to an abrupt halt when a thirty-eight special made its appearance from inside the black jacket. Jeff thought maybe he should have omitted the "you idiot!" from his last sentence. He somehow fumbled through an explanation about how he had no idea she had a boyfriend—"Just a misunderstanding. No need to get carried away, pal." He kept pushing at the air with the palms of his hands in a "calm the fuck down" motion.

"Red" ditched him on the spot to run off with the gun-slinging lout. As he watched them speed off, the last visual he had of his date was her straddling the back of a Harley Davidson with her dress hiked up to her crotch. He thought to himself, thank God I don't have to kiss her goodnight!

But as he jumped into his car and headed for home, he began to feel something not quite right on the seat of his pants. He hadn't even realized that he had sat in a humungous wad of wet, sticky, bubble gum in the theater (her gum?) and it was now deeply infused into the seat of his brand new "Zanella" dress slacks. He reached under his butt and pulled at the slimy glob that was now stuck to his pants, his car seat and his fingers. It reminded him of that melted cheese that just keeps stringing and stringing no matter how far you pull the damn stuff. No, he was not ready for dating just yet.

CHAPTER 2

He was to meet Kevin outside the main door so they could make their entrance together. He couldn't, for the life of him, figure out why Kevin was so insistent on having this big support system just to go to a company party. Perhaps it was because the place was so ritzy. Kevin was in his element in a casual setting where he mixed, hobnobbed with strangers, shamelessly flirted with all of the cute girls—but this was different. This was uptown stuff. He was terribly intrigued with high-class functions, but needed his buddy at his side for a while—until he could get his feet wet and start to mingle with this crowd. Jeff reminded him that these were just employees at the same company where he worked, but Kevin told him they seemed real different dressed in black tie and evening gowns at this swanky club.

After Jeff handed over his keys to the valet, he spotted Kevin standing by the main entrance—blatantly checking his watch. "I'm only ten minutes late, you simpleton. It takes time to put on all these layers of clothes," he said, indicating his three-piece suit.

"I've been here for twenty minutes. I was gonna kill you if you didn't show."

"You want me to hold your hand, dear?"

"Shut-up, asshole," Kevin shot back. "I wasn't going in there alone. But I'll tell you one thing—these chicks are unreal! I've been standing here scoping them out as they walk in. I was right. The place is crawlin' with stag chicks."

"Oh goodie!"

"You dork."

"Let's go in and find a table. I haven't had two bites of food all day."

"Well, they have cocktails for an hour before they serve dinner," Kevin informed.

"Great. Martinis on an empty stomach."

"Are you gonna be belly aching all night?"

"If I suck my cheeks in maybe they'll feel sorry for me and give me an extra olive."

They made their way through the crowds of people toward the bar, but a gentleman with a tray of hors d'oeuvres intercepted them. He offered a variety of yummy looking eats. Both men shamelessly helped themselves to several.

"May I offer you gentlemen a cocktail?" he asked.

"Oh yeah," Kevin replied. "Scotch rocks for me and what…a martini for my friend here."

"Very well, sir." He turned and gave their drink order to another waiter. Super classy!

"Isn't this some joint?" Kevin raved.

"It's plush. I could get used to this. How about you?"

"In a New York minute."

"So the higher ups in the company are members here, huh?"

"Yeah. Lucky sons o' bitches. Someday Jeffrey….we'll be hittin' it down the fairway out there. Just you wait an' see."

"Keep dreamin' my friend. I've heard that the memberships here go for a mere three hundred grand plus yearly dues. Think you can scrape that together?"

"Gotta have goals." His eyes scanned the crowd. "Like that foxy little blond over there… talking to her girlfriend. That's for me. Her girlfriend—that's for you."

"Thank you, but I'll do my own shopping."

Just then the waiter came to deliver their libation order. "Scotch rocks and martini up," he said as he handed each of them their drink along with a cocktail napkin. "Thank you gentlemen," he said as he turned and disappeared into the crowd.

"Were we supposed to tip him?" Kevin asked.

"I don't think so," Jeff guessed. "Isn't this whole thing paid for by your company?"

"Yeah, the whole kit and kaboodle."

"Okay then. Your boss must give them all a tip at the end of the night."

"I'd hate to see the bill for this shindig. I'd need bank financing just for the goddamned tips. Hey, did you see that? The lights just flashed. That must mean they want people to find a table. How about over there. It's right next to the band and the dance floor."

"Did you bring cotton?"

"For what?"

"For my ears when they fire up that band and we're sitting right in front of those eighteen-inch woofers."

"You are such a pussy! Well, where do you wanna sit?"

"How about over there," Jeff said, pointing to a table a few rows back and to the side.

"Okay, okay. Over there."

Dinner consisted of soup and salad; then chicken piccata with whipped potatoes and asparagus with hollandaise sauce. Two bottles of fine wine graced each table—one white and one red. Dessert was a warm chocolate chip cookie topped with rich, vanilla ice cream.

After the tables were cleared, the lights softened and the band started up. People immediately left their seats and crowded the dance floor and the aisles to mix with friends and introduce themselves to strangers. The bar area was overflowing with guests ordering drinks and engaging in conversations.

Kevin made a beeline to invite the blond he had singled out to join him on the dance floor. Jeff ended up sitting all by himself at the large round table. After people watching for a time, he left his seat and headed to the bar to freshen his martini. The bar was three deep with people frantically taking full advantage of the hosted bar, but he finally was served after shouting his order over people's heads five times before grabbing the attention of one of the bartenders.

As he started pushing his way back through the swarm of bodies, a young woman turned into him with such force, she spilled her fresh Black Russian all over his jacket, vest, shirt and tie. The impact also sent his martini flying from the glass to join forces with her drink in midair. He stood facing her, the syrupy Kailua, vodka and gin dripping down his entire front.

"I'm so sorry. Somebody pushed me and I couldn't stop myself. It was that guy walking away. He didn't even apologize. Can you believe it?"

"It's okay. Don't worry about it." What was it with him and women?

"Please," she begged. "Let me get some club soda from the bartender. I can get most of that out before it sets."

She left him standing there but returned in a few minutes with a tall glass of club soda and three bar towels in hand. "Let's get out of the line of fire here before it happens again." She led him off to the side where there weren't many people.

As she began her blotting and wiping frenzy, Jeff really looked at her for the first time. She was quite striking with soft brown hair that fell in huge, bouncy waves halfway down her back, eyes that matched her hair perfectly and model type bone structure covered by a flawless complexion. Not too much make-up, he noticed. A natural beauty. His eyes drifted to her voluptuous body. Firm breasts a bit out of proportion with the rest of her slender figure. She was wearing a black, flowing pants suit topped with a mauve colored, tailored jacket. Very stylish.

"There. I think I got most of it out. You're pretty wet, huh?" Jeff nodded and could not stop the grin that was tugging at the corners of his mouth. She flashed him a solid smile. "Oh, by the way, my name is Shawna Reese."

"Jeff Daniels," he answered, extending his right hand.

She took his hand sheepishly and said, "Not the best of circumstances, but it's nice to meet you, Jeff."

"I just hope I don't get pulled over on the way home," he said surveying the damage. "They'll lock me up for sure."

"I'll come and bail you out," she promised.

"Don't worry about it. I'm a magnet for anything wet or sticky. Happens all the time."

"Where are you sitting?"

"Over on the other side. My girlfriend's dancing and everyone else left the table. Where's your table?"

"Right here," he said, pointing to the table in the corner. "Would you care to join me? I got deserted too."

"Sure."

He escorted her to his table and pulled out the chair next to his for her to sit down. "You work at this company?"

"Yes. I work in inventory. What department are you in?"

"Oh, I don't work for McCormick. I'm just here with a friend. He works there as a salesman. I work at Mattel Toy Company."

"What do you do?"

"I design toys."

"No kidding. What a great job."

"It has its moments. They expect brilliant ideas all the time. Then I'm always under the gun to get a prototype worked up so that it can be tested on the kids. If it checks out, then it goes to manufacturing. If it doesn't, it's back to square one either making improvements on that toy or scrapping the project and starting on something new."

"So sometimes the kids give it the thumbs down?"

"Sometimes."

"That is a pressure job."

"Well, when things go well, it can be pretty creative. Rewarding. I started with Mattel right out of college."

She seemed very sweet. Jeff noticed a little shyness about her—a bit of insecurity maybe. He kind of liked that about her. Brash women turned him off—ones that made a man feel bulldozed. This woman was quite the opposite. Soft. Intriguing.

They sat and talked for the rest of the evening. Kevin came back to the table several times to catch his breath and take a few swigs of his scotch. Then he'd be off again to mingle and dance with the foxy blond who had caught his eye. With the help of a little alcohol, his reservations about this posh country club had melted into oblivion. He looked like his old self again.

Jeff had to admit to himself that the evening wasn't turning out to be such a bust after all. Shawna was so different—nice to talk to. But one thing he did notice about her, every time he asked something about her, she made some vague response and then turned the conversation back to being all about him. Not that he minded talking about himself, but it was a bit odd after all of the garrulous women he had met lately.

He ended up telling her his life story. He told her how he had met Kevin and what good friends they were. All about the tumultuous home in which he had grown up. His eleven brothers and sisters. His absentee parents.

"So, you didn't even have a room to yourself growing up?"

"Are you kidding? I had to share a bedroom with two of my brothers," he began his digression. "One of them was terrified of the dark—couldn't sleep without a light on. The other one couldn't sleep if even one sliver of light was detectable."

"Whoa, that must have wreaked havoc on your serenity at bedtime, huh?"

"Serenity?" he spouted off. "Ricky kept switching on the closet light—then Bentley would jump up and shut it off. They kept going at it like this until they broke the damn light chain. Then mom gave Ricky a night-light that plugged in to the socket. This started a new war with Ricky plugging it in and Bentley yanking it back out."

"Did it ever escalate to blows?"

"All the time," he told her. "I thought they were gonna kill each other, the neurotic little shits."

"This went on every night?"

"Every goddamned night!" Suddenly remembering with whom he was speaking, he back peddled right away. "I'm sorry, Shawna. See how worked up I still get?"

"It's perfectly okay," she smiled. "Which one would win the fights?"

"Sometimes Ricky would win. Then, Bentley would mash his pillow into his face to block out the light. I'd get worried that he was gonna smother himself, but every time I tried to pull the pillow off, he'd start taking swings at me!"

"What happened when Bentley won?"

"Then Ricky would go downstairs to sleep in the living room with the lamp on."

"I'm just curious… how did they both turn out?"

"Bentley's gay and Ricky's a stuntman for the studios."

Shawna shook her head as she exploded into a gut laugh. "So that's how you know so much about toys… because of all those little brothers and sisters?"

"Yep. I know what kids will go for. If there's one thing growing up with that litter taught me, it was what to give 'em to play with to keep 'em occupied and out of my hair for a while. Hey, I've talked your ear off," he apologized. "I haven't learned one thing about you."

"I like hearing about you," she said.

"Where do you live?" he asked.

"I have an apartment in the valley."

"How about having dinner with me sometime?" he ventured.

"Sometime… I guess that'd be okay."

That'd be okay? he thought. *What a peculiar answer.*

CHAPTER 3

Jeff called her mid-week in hopes to set up a date for next Saturday. The conversation was brief—just enough for her to give her address and directions to her apartment.

"Seven o'clock?"

"Okay. Bye."

"Bye," he answered taken aback by her abrupt ending to the phone call. He had hoped to chat a little—find out more about her.

When he picked her up, she answered the door completely ready with her purse in her hand—slipping out of the door, immediately shutting it behind her.

"Do you have a roommate?" he asked thinking maybe someone was inside who was not decent to receive guests.

"No."

He waited for an explanation for the odd reception, but she said nothing so he continued, "You live alone?" *What a stupid question,* he thought. *She just said she didn't have a roommate.*

"Yes. I live by myself. How about you? Do you have an apartment?"

Oh good! He could take some time answering her question and fill in the awkwardness that was already beginning to invade the conversation. He let her in the passenger side door, walked around, got in and pulled out onto the street. "I have a house in Calabasas. Three bedrooms, three baths with a great view of the valley. I bought it six years ago when the company gave me a real decent raise."

"Wow. You were only twenty-four when you bought it, huh?"

"Yeah. I consider myself real lucky to be where I'm at with my career. I pretty much have everything I want. It's a comfortable feeling. And you?"

"I have no complaints."

They drove in awkward silence until Jeff pulled up to the valet at Oscar's, his favorite seafood restaurant. His stomach was beginning to rumble from hunger with a bit of nervousness mixed in. He hoped she wasn't noticing.

The hostess seated them in a cozy booth in the corner where they pondered the menu together. Thank God, something to talk about. Jeff recommended a few entrees that he loved, then they ordered.

"So, do you have a family?" he asked.

"A family? You mean a husband and kids or parents and siblings?"

"Parents and siblings," he laughed. "You don't have a husband and kids do you?"

"No." Her smile widened. "My father died two years ago and my mother and my seventeen-year-old brother live in Grants Pass, Oregon."

"Oregon. That's a beautiful state. What brought you to sunny California?"

"The sun," she laughed. "And you told me a little about your family the other night. All those kids. Do they all live in California?"

"Some of them are still home with mom and dad. Some are all spread out over the country now."

Despite hard work and searching his mind madly for anything to say—any damn thing at all—the conversation kept slipping into what felt like long-lasting blank spaces. Dead air. This was making

Jeff's stomach "rock and roll" even louder. At least it seemed loud to him. And if he could hear it from where he was sitting, then she certainly must. Where was that damn waiter?

Finally, the waiter brought their salads and they started to eat; however, a family with two small children had just been seated across from them. The parents were looking at the menu. Jeff kept looking over there out of the corner of his eye. From the time the family sat down, the oldest kid (looked about three) was yelling some stupid kid limerick over and over and over. The youngest one was beating his spoon on the high chair tray. Annoyed, Jeff kept shooting malevolent stares in their direction, but they did not notice or seem to care that their "little dears" were disrupting the entire restaurant.

"You get together on holidays?" Shawna blurted, trying to divert Jeff's mind from the racket across the way.

"What?" he said, snapping his attention back to his date. "We do now," he answered as he continued to flash his worst dirty looks to the parents. Shawna noticed others eyeing them with distain as well. "For a while, I didn't even want to be with the family. I was so burned out and pissed off. I made peace with my parents a couple of years ago and now I can tolerate the get-togethers... as long as they're few and far between..."

He trailed off and waved for the manager to come to their table. "You need to do something to shut those brats up. It's plain the parents don't give a damn whose dinner they ruin."

"I'm sorry sir. Would you care to be seated at another table?"

"What good would that do? You can hear that clamor all over the restaurant."

"That's all I can offer you, sir. Their waiter has spoken to them, but they're customers as well."

"Well, you just lost these two," Jeff bellowed as he threw a twenty-dollar bill down on the table. *Enough to more than cover the salads,* he thought.

The waiter had just arrived with their bottle of wine—hadn't been opened yet. "Come on Shawna, let's get out of here."

When they got back into the car, Jeff turned to her, "I put up with that all my life until I left for college… that noise… that yelling. I'll be damned if I'm gonna let two outta control brats spoil our night."

"Wow! You really don't like children, do you?" she said with eyes wide.

"It's a sore spot. Hey, I know a quiet place. Marcello's. It's not far from here either."

Colossal mistake! As the hostess led them through the restaurant, there was Amber and her new heartthrob—right smack next to the table where the girl had put their menus down. There the four of them were, face to face. It was impossible to pretend he didn't see them. They were right there. "Hi, Jeff," Amber shot a sheepish smile as she looked up from her little cup of soup. They're only on their soup, Jeff's mind raced. *I can't ask the hostess to put us at a different table. We're standing right in front of them. This is goddamned awkward!*

If he'd only stopped to think, he might have guessed that they would run into Amber at Marcello's. This had been one of their regular haunts when they were together. Good restaurants—one of the few things they had enjoyed in common. "Oh wow," he said shaking his head. "This is a surprise." He turned to his date in order to present her to his girlfriend. "Well… this is… this is…" Total blank. *You idiot!* he thought, *you know her goddamned name… it's, it's…*

"Shawna," she broke in to rescue Jeff from his lapse in memory.

"This is Drew… I'm Amber," she interjected. No one was extending any hands—like four people with frontal lobotomies. Then Amber looked directly at Jeff, "How've you been anyway?"

"Oh… fine, fine," he answered with a lazy, cynical tone.

"Well, it's nice to see you. Enjoy your dinner. Good to meet you… ah…?"

"Shawna… nice to meet you too. Nice to meet you, Drew."

"Same here."

They slid into their booth, which allowed a good three feet between them and Amber and her computer-matched dickhead. Jeff watched as the couple's heads instantly went together—whispering back and forth into one another's ear—evidently discussing the embarrassing situation because Drew's eyes kept glancing up to grab another look at the pathetic jerk Amber had dumped for him.

"That an Ex?" Shawna asked in a hushed voice.

"Uh huh."

"Her new boyfriend?"

"Apparently."

Jeff tried to push against Shawna as far as he could for his seating position placed him staring straight into "Drew's" face—and they were only on their soup!

Struggling to keep his eyes from wandering over "there," he tried to appear comfortable and in control of the situation. Like it was no big deal. No big deal, ha! He couldn't help but wonder if they were getting down to business in their "baby making" endeavor. Couldn't get the graphic picture of this out of his mind. The two of them seemed to be engaged in an animated conversation—all chummy and shit—like they'd been together a lot longer than three months.

The food was probably good—Italian; however, besides the insanity of sitting right next to Amber and Mr. Computerhead, Jeff still felt that he had to work to keep any kind of conversation going with Shawna. Was Amber noticing the long pauses in the conversation between him and his date? At least he was glad that Shawna looked ravishing—that'd show her. After they left the restaurant, (right on the heels of Amber and Drew), he could think of nothing else to do and she certainly wasn't forthcoming with any suggestions, so he drove her home. In truth, the entire evening was taking it's toll on his nerves—between walking out of Oscar's, running into Amber and the strain of trying to pull two sentences out of his date, all he really wanted now was to go home, watch "Seinfeld" and go to bed.

He walked her to her door where they stood uncomfortably facing each other. Jeff waited for an invitation to come in, but all she did was stand there—staring off into space. He leaned forward and gave her a peck on her cheek, but even this innocent gesture made her stiffen. Christ, what was with this girl?

"I don't know, Kev. I think she's just not into me." Jeff described the latest installment of his dating disasters to Kevin who after wails of laughter over his buddy's unfortunate encounter with the old girlfriend, was sizing up the situation. The two had met at Pedro's, their favorite Mexican restaurant, after work the next evening.

"Either that or she's real shy," Kevin offered.

"Why didn't she invite me in?"

"Maybe she's afraid of you."

"Ya think?"

"You look pretty scary to me."

"Shut-up."

"Are you gonna ask her out again?"

"No. I don't think so," Jeff alleged. "Something was wrong. I've never met anyone like her before. I'm definitely attracted to her but I get the feeling she's hiding something…ya know?"

"She sounds kinda bazaar to me. Maybe you better steer clear. Ya never know what you're gettin' yourself into."

"Too bad. I really thought I'd hit the jackpot with this one—fate maybe. Hey, did you go out with that blond you were trying to pick up? What was her name—Sandra?"

"Emily," he corrected. "I'll tell ya, I spent a wad on dinner and that show at the Music Center…Chicago. When I brought her home, she asked me in for a drink, but as soon as I walked in an' saw a gigantic picture of Jesus Christ above her mantle, I knew I wasn't gonna get lucky."

Jeff tried to put Shawna out of his mind in the weeks that followed. He was glad that he had a pressing project to finish. He was deeply engrossed in a remote controlled set of action figures that walked around like little robots when his secretary popped her head in.

"A note came for you, Jeff—along with a box of something that smells luscious." Ginny handed him the delivery and watched him with anticipation.

"Are you gonna open it?"

"Who gave it to you?" he asked.

"A very attractive brunette," she said, unable to stifle the grin that was overtaking her face.

"You're kidding. Is she still here?"

"No. She handed me the box and the note, said it was for Jeff Daniels, then turned right around and left the office."

"Sorry Ginny, I think I'm gonna need some privacy for this one." He opened the door with a wide gesture of his arm showing her the way out.

He sat down and tore open the note first. "Jeff, I hope you don't mind that I showed up at your work but I didn't hear from you after our date and I don't have your phone number. I just want you to know that it was the best date I've ever been on. I thought we were connecting really well. I hope I'm not being too forward in asking you over to dinner this Saturday night. I'm making chicken stroganoff over noodles. Sound good? About seven? Let me know. You have my number. Shawna. P.S. Enjoy the cookies."

Stunned, he opened the box and stared at home made, chocolate chip and pecan cookies. He immediately picked one out and put it into his mouth. Yum! He took the box out to Ginny's office and set it on her desk.

"Cute and she makes a hell of a cookie."

She looked up at him with an ear-to-ear grin. "Is this a keeper?"

"Don't know yet. Maybe though." He smiled back.

CHAPTER 4

So I actually get invited inside the apartment tonight, he thought on his drive into the valley. This girl was certainly an enigma. Why had she not invited him in that first night, at least when he first arrived? That was just etiquette. Maybe her place was a mess or maybe there was something she didn't want him to see. The mystery building in his mind, he just had to find out why she was so taciturn about herself. What was she hiding anyway?

She told him to be casual so he wore beige pants and a soft, jade colored short sleeve shirt. When she opened the door, she looked fetching in her rose-colored Capri's and pale pink blouse. Her hair was pulled up on the sides and held with a clip at the crown, then falling loosely past her shoulders and down her back. Totally sexy.

"So, you couldn't resist the entrée being served, huh?"

"No. I couldn't resist the cook."

She invited him in and gestured for him to sit down on the sofa. Soft music was playing on the stereo.

His eyes scanned the room. It was quite charming having the look of a professional decorator's touch. The sofa and matching chair were traditional style covered in very expensive looking, muted green, lavender and mauve upholstery. The coffee table and end tables were rosewood with inlaid green and beige marble. The lamps appeared to be antiques that put him in mind of his paternal grandmother's house back in Springfield, Missouri. The lights were set low, creating a nice, mellow atmosphere.

His eyes traveled to the dining area where he spotted an elegant mahogany dinette with matching china cabinet. The cabinet was impeccably decorated with gorgeous antique china and gold rimmed wine and champagne glasses. The entire place was tastefully done. The scene pleased Jeff as his mind journeyed back in time to when Amber had first moved in with him. She had quickly revealed herself to be a major slob leaving piles of magazines, old newspapers, manicuring paraphernalia, shoes, clothes etc. all over his house. When he tried to tidy up, she would bark, "Leave that stuff alone—I'm not done with it yet!"

"You have a beautiful apartment. Did you hire a decorator?"

"I did it myself, but thanks for the compliment."

"You are a very talented lady," he smiled. She returned an embarrassed grin.

"I have the makings for a martini. I seem to recall that being your drink of choice."

"Now, how did you remember that?" he teased.

"It's permanently embedded in my brain…and probably your suit."

She mixed a drink for him and one for herself. Handing him his martini, she sat in a chair opposite him. The conversation was once again strained—neither knowing quite how to start a comfortable flow. Then Shawna asked what his current toy project was. This got him going and he filled her in on the action figures that moved by remote control. Some of them were the bad guys—real ugly, and some were the heroes—strong and handsome. She hung on every word and they ended up laughing and talking with a lot more ease. The conversation moved on to Jeff's little brothers and sisters once again and there was no end to the tales he had to tell.

"Hungry?" she finally asked.

"Famished. It smells incredible."

"Come on, sit." She showed him to his chair at the table where she served an impressively tasty meal. After dinner and several more drinks each, Jeff asked her to dance.

"Oh, I really don't dance. Two left feet, you know."

"Is that why I never saw you on the dance floor at the party? Cause I know you must have been asked."

"I feel awkward trying to dance. I know I look foolish. Like people are laughing at me."

"That's all in your imagination. No one's laughing—trust me." He held out his hand in an invitation to join him on the living room carpet. Shawna felt cornered so she stood and took his hand. She was trembling.

"Are you nervous?" he laughed.

"I really am. I don't like being on the spot."

He lifted her chin and gazed deeply into her timid, brown eyes. "You're not on the spot, Shawna. We all need to push through our fears. You know, step out of our comfort zones. I'll take care of you. I promise."

She smiled but could not hide her uneasiness.

"Just follow me. Don't even think about the steps," he reassured her.

Jeff took her firmly into his arms and they danced around the entire room, from one end of the dining room through every square inch of the living room and back again. She began to relax into his protective caress—a brand new sensation for her.

Overcome with his desires, he tightened his arms around her and pulled her body close to his. He gently leaned down to kiss her lips when he felt her body stiffen as she pushed him away with force.

"What's the matter? Why the mixed signals?"

"I… I'm just too nervous. I don't know what to do."

"Why in the world are you afraid of me? Am I that scary looking?"

"Of course not. It's just… it's just that…."

"That what?" he implored, his frustration beginning to show.

"I'm a virgin," she blurted out, both hands quickly flying up to cover her mouth. She had not intended to reveal anything personal… not yet. It must be the drinks that were causing her to lose her composure.

Jeff looked at her in stunned silence. They locked eyes as she returned his stare.

After a time, he sat down on the sofa and put his hands over his face, his fingers rubbing back and forth through his eyebrows.

"I'm sorry," she finally spoke.

He looked up with a sweet smile. "What are you sorry for? I think it's wonderful. I'm just amazed. How old are you anyway?"

She hesitated. "Twenty-five."

"Well, that's quite an accomplishment for twenty-five. Are you very religious?"

"No. I'm not religious at all."

"Then why… how? I shouldn't be asking you this."

"I've never had a boyfriend."

"Get out! A sweet girl who looks like you? That doesn't add up."

But, the look in her eyes confirmed that she was telling the truth.

"How come you agreed to go out with me?"

"I sensed something real special in you. You were so understanding when I drenched you with all that icky stuff. You're so different from any guy I've ever met."

"You need to get out more."

She laughed. "Jeff."

"Uh huh?"

"I really want you to kiss me."

He looked at her with apprehension, then took her into his arms and placed his lips softly against hers. He could feel a battle stirring up in her body. She became rigid; however, he could clearly sense her desire for him.

She put her arms around his neck and kissed him back…an inexperienced kiss. He pulled her closer and allowed his tongue to find hers. She seemed edgy and excited at the same time. When he released his hold, she was actually shaky.

"You all right?" he asked with genuine concern.

"Oh yes. Wow!" she exclaimed, allowing her body to collapse onto the sofa.

"You've never kissed a man before either?"

"Not like that."

On Jeff's drive home, his rational mind was waging war with his carnal desires. "Jesus, she's hot," he said to himself. "But this is too damn much responsibility. I've never been the first with anyone." His good sense told him to back off from this situation—that there was more than meets the eye going on with this girl. After all, what did he know about her? About her past? Not one damn thing. He decided to take some time to think it over.

CHAPTER 5

The more Jeff tried to push thoughts of Shawna out of his mind, the more they kept popping back in. He was even having trouble sleeping. *What if she were next to me right now?* he pondered. *How would I get her to relax and trust me? I know there's a lot of pain for women the first time.*

He continued picturing this scene all different ways. He was driving himself crazy. *What could it hurt to pursue her?* he thought. *It either works itself out or it doesn't. She doesn't seem like the woman in "Fatal Attraction" or anything.*

After confiding his situation to Kevin, he sat back in his chair at Pedro's to gain his buddy's brilliant insight.

"This is weird. I agree that somethin's going on with her that's not quite right. Was she hurt big time in her past that makes her so jumpy with men?"

"I don't know. She doesn't say much about her past."

"Have you asked her right out if she'd been hurt?" Kevin probed as he was annoyingly beating out a drum cadence on the tabletop.

"No. I can't figure out a way to smoothly work that into the conversation," Jeff replied. "She's so closed up. She seems remarkably innocent for a woman of twenty- five."

"There's somethin' abnormal here. It's not worth getting involved. I think you should shine this one, pal."

"But she's sweet…and really cute."

"The world's full of cute chicks who aren't off the deep end."

Ignoring all of Kevin's advice, Jeff called her a few weeks later. "I noticed you have some great antiques in your place. Do you like to go antiquing?"

"I love to go antiquing! That's my favorite thing. That and movies."

Jeff was delighted for these were also his favorite indulgences. Amber had always had a hard time sitting through a movie and was blatantly vocal about her hatred of antiques. "Why would anyone want that old used junk?" she would ask him. "It just clutters up the house." He was forced to admit now that he really had very little in common with Amber. With almost every, single activity in which they participated, one of them was making an extreme concession to the other.

He picked Shawna up and this time she invited him in. It was a warm, summer day and Shawna was wearing a pair of yellow shorts with a matching yellow and white tank top. She looked very enticing. Jeff had also worn a pair of white shorts that hit his legs just above his knees and a black T-shirt with a silk-screened picture of Duffy on the front.

"Is that your dog?" she asked, smiling at the shaggy little face on Jeff's shirt.

"Yeah. This is Duffy, my cairn terrier. He's my best buddy in the world."

"He's adorable! I love dogs."

"My buddy, Kevin, says he looks like something that should've been dry cleaned but was washed."

Shawna laughed out loud, "I wish they would allow pets in my building. I really miss having the pitter-patter of paws around the house. I had a dog when I was home with my mom, but she died of cancer a few months before I moved to Los Angeles. She was old—seventeen, but I still can't get used to not having her with me. She slept in my bed every night for all those years."

Lucky dog, Jeff thought.

They had a fantastic day together. Jeff took her to lunch, then they drove to a place in the city where there was street after street of nothing but antique shops. They browsed. They bought. And they had no lapses in conversation on this day. Shawna was up and bubbly and full of information about the items they were looking at. She really knew her antiques.

Jeff knew a little but was amazed by the extent of her knowledge. He was full of questions and she was excited to fill him in on just about anything he wanted to know.

"How about a movie next Saturday night?" he asked when he walked her to her door. It was dark by this time and he was prepared for a peck on the cheek—then he would say good night. No use pushing it after they had had such an awesome day.

"I'd love to. What kind of movies do you like?"

"You pick," he said as he leaned towards her to give a good night cheek kiss. But he felt her hands come up to caress his face so he let her take charge. He never knew what to expect with Shawna. Her lips tentatively met his and he kissed her with all of the warmth and affection that he was clearly feeling. They parted briefly, then kissed again. The feelings in Jeff's body were new. As much as he had loved Amber, the emotions he had felt when he held her were nothing like what he was feeling now. The chemistry with Shawna was electric.

When they released their embrace, they gazed deeply into each other's eyes. At this perfect moment, there was nothing to be said. Jeff simply whispered, "Good night."

"Good night," she responded. She went in and he turned and walked back to his car.

CHAPTER 6

The next weeks were filled with dinners, lunches, movies and antiquing. Jeff had a nagging feeling that there was a lot he did not know about Shawna, but he was powerless to stay away from her, even for a weekend.

When he finally met Kevin for happy hour one Wednesday night, he was surprised by the tongue-lashing he received. "You're off with Little Red Riding Hood and you don't have time for your friends anymore."

"Hey, I'm sorry, man. I didn't know you cared that much. I'm flattered."

"Fuck you. So what's the latest on the ice cube—fill me in," Kevin said as he waved his hand towards himself in a 'come on, tell' gesture.

"Well… we've been spending a ton of time together. This whole thing has my head reeling. I'll tell you, I've never felt like this before. I think I'm falling, Kev."

"Have you done the deed yet?"

"Nope. Only kissing so far."

"Great party that was—a virgin and a born again Christian. How long you gonna wait for the ice to melt… ten years?"

"You are such an asshole. She's not cold. She's just innocent… shy… I think."

"Or something," Kevin replied with suspicion easily readable in his eyes.

"Or maybe she just cares who she gives her body to. Ever thought of that?"

"I really hope you know what you're doing. I don't have a good feeling about this. There's something she's not telling you. Something big."

"How do you know?"

"Just a sense. I'm usually right about these things."

"You're usually right about diddly squat."

"Suit yourself. Just don't come cryin' to me when your little heart gets broke."

"You can count on it."

"How about if I cook dinner for you this time?" Jeff asked Shawna on a mid-week phone call.

"At your house?"

"Well, I wasn't about to invade your kitchen. Yes, my house. Saturday night. Say 'yes Mr. Daniels, I'd love to.'"

"Yes, Mr. Daniels, I'd love to," she giggled.

"Pick you up at six-thirty?"

"Oh, you don't have to drive all the way over here to pick me up. I'll be happy to drive to your place."

He gave her the address and directions and asked if poached salmon would be okay. She made and "mmmm" sound, then they said good-bye.

Following his directions, she drove up into the hills and turned left onto a street named "Royal View Ridge." She thought the neighborhood was startlingly beautiful with tall evergreens lining both sides of the street. All of the homes were impeccably kept, displaying the most artistic landscaping. Each house was custom-built, some two-story, some single-story ranch style—all on oversized lots.

Driving slowly, she crept up to the given address of 5629 and parked in front. So this is Jeff's home, she reveled. A sprawling, one story nestled into a richly wooded lot. It had soft gray wooden siding with white trim on the windows and shutters. The charming flower lined walkway led to a grand, double door—white with stained glass inlay. She pressed the bell.

At six-thirty sharp, Jeff opened the door to see Shawna standing there with a bottle of Chardonnay in hand. She looked especially beautiful in a form fitting; lavender dress that only a woman with her figure could pull off. And she pulled it off to the absolute max.

"Welcome. Do come in," he said making a wide, swooping gesture with his arm. As soon as she stepped into the foyer, she felt something wet pushing against her leg.

"This is Duffy. My better half."

"Oh, he's so cute. He looks like 'Toto.'"

"I know. He's the same breed—a cairn terrier."

She handed him the bottle and stooped down to cuddle the squirming little dog. Jeff put the bottle in the refrigerator, then came back and stood above her.

"Come on. I'll show you the house—then we can eat. This is the living room," he said beginning his grand tour. As she stood up, her eyes were filled with the most stunning house she had ever seen. She moved out of the marble foyer and stepped down into an elegant living room where the mauve carpet was a dramatic background to the strikingly white, upholstered sofa and love seat. The large stone fireplace stood proudly with life-sized statues of golfers on either side—a man on the right and a lady on the left—each leaning on their golf club with a ball at their feet. The mantle was adorned with antique artifacts and a bronze bust of Beethoven. She heard soft piano and strings coming from a Bose system—the speakers strategically placed throughout the room and the rest of the house, she was about to find out. Plants and colorful flowers were creatively added to the extraordinary scene.

"Oh, my God. This is spectacular!"

"I did hire a professional decorator," he admitted. She laughed, then he showed her through the rest of the residence. Her eyes drank in the fabulous kitchen—huge with a center island and dark, hard wood flooring and cabinets. The walls were wainscoted with hand rubbed mahogany on the bottom half and white, turquoise and taupe ivy patterned wallpaper that rose to the ceiling.

The master bedroom made a bold statement with heavy pieces of rosewood and mahogany. She almost swooned as she gazed at the four-poster bed with a patchwork quilt with tan and sage throw pillows on top. The bathrooms were marble with rose and gray colored wallpaper in the master, and a tan and mauve pattern in the guests.

He showed two exquisite guest bedrooms and a den where there was a big screen TV and shelves that were overflowing with photos of his family members. Her eyes fell on a large; teak framed oil painting of all fourteen of them together mounted over yet another charming fireplace.

"So this is everybody?" she asked.

"That's the whole brood plus mom and dad."

"How did you get them all to hold still for a portrait?"

"It was actually painted from a photo. The kids would never have sat still to pose for a painting." He chuckled—just the thought of it.

"God, I still can't get over fourteen people in one house," she exclaimed.

"Fourteen people and two bathrooms."

"How in the world did you do that?"

"I don't know. My sisters would spend hours in there getting ready and I'll tell you, when they came out, they didn't look any different than when they went in. I couldn't count the number of times I had to hoof it down to the corner gas station to use the facilities. All of the boys in my family got to know the attendants on a first name basis. We were down there so much, I'm surprised the plumbing held up for all those years."

Jeff always made Shawna laugh so hard with his crazy family stories. "When am I going to meet this brood?"

"You actually want to be subjected to that?"

"Sure. Why not?"

"Bring your ear plugs."

Shawna shot him a dubious grin. "You really do love them, don't you?"

"I do. But I can only take them all together in small doses." He turned and looked into her brown eyes. "I'm flattered that you want to meet my family."

"Your house is so beautiful… so flawless," she raved, still looking around—carefully inspecting every little nuance. "It's the most breath-taking place I've ever seen."

"All my life, growing up, I lived in utter chaos. As fast as I'd put things away, the kids were pulling 'em out again. It was a demoralizing battle and I finally surrendered to the upheaval. So that's why I went a little overboard with my own home."

"I love it. I'm a nut about having a perfect home too. My house, growing up, was very pedestrian… actually, to be honest, it was a dump!"

He laughed and she joined in.

Jeff picked up Duffy who had been sticking to them like glue throughout the tour—checking out this new and intriguing guest. "Whata' you say Duff, shall we feed this poor, starving girl?" He kissed the little dog on the head then put him back down.

He showed her to her seat at the dining room table where he had created a mood with candlelight and beautifully set china and crystal. He served poached salmon topped with hollandaise sauce, asparagus and boiled red potatoes. He poured the chilled Chardonnay that she had brought. Dessert was hot apple pie topped with vanilla ice cream.

"This pie is out of this world!" she exclaimed.

"One of my sisters baked it. She's an incredible cook, but desserts are her forte."

After dinner, Jeff quickly threw everything into the dishwasher and poured another glass of wine for each of them. "Come on. Let's go sit under the stars and enjoy the view for a while."

When Shawna stepped out of the back door, she almost toppled over when she caught sight of the sea of lights below. The evening was warm and clear with subtle gusts of summer breezes. He ushered her to sit down in one of four white, wicker chairs that pushed up to a matching glass topped table where he set their glasses of wine along with a newly opened bottle. "Oh my God, you have a view of the whole valley. This is awesome!"

"Romantic, huh?"

She looked over at him. "Very. What a gorgeous home you have, Jeff. I've never seen anything like this in my whole life. You must be so happy here."

"I'm really lucky to have this. I never take it for granted—not for one minute. I went to work for Mattel right out of college and they've been super to me. I love my work and I love my home."

"And your dog," she said as she leaned over to pick up Duffy.

"And my dog."

"Did you get him from a breeder?"

"Yeah. Amber, the one we ran into at Marcello's that night. She and I bought him together, but he and I bonded so close that she gave me full custody when she left. She gets no visitation."

"She lived here with you?"

"Uh huh, for the last year of our relationship. I think she bought a condo with her new boyfriend a few months ago."

"How do you know that?"

"She called me the next day—after we saw them. She went on and on about how embarrassing that was—then she asked me what I thought of Drew."

"Well… what did you think of him?"

"Personally... I thought he looked like a dork—probably an airhead. What did you think?" he asked, probing for a second opinion—one that would hopefully support his own.

"He was okay looking... not very friendly though."

"Well, I really hope she's happy. She says she is—I don't know. But that's ancient history. Tell me about you. About your family."

"I just got a call from my mother before I came over. She's been battling cancer for two years. She's been feeling real weak and tired for a long time now so they did more tests. It's in her liver. She says it's terminal."

"Oh, I'm so sorry. Are you all right? You must feel terrible."

"I do, but I've known it was serious for a long time. I could tell by the way she was going down hill. I'm gonna go see her next week. I wanna spend as much time with her as I can. Help her with things."

"She's not alone, is she? I mean, your brother's there with her, isn't he?"

Jeff noticed the most peculiar look come over Shawna's face.

"Yes... but... I... I need to be there."

"Oh, of course you do. I didn't mean to imply that... you have to go. She needs to see you too. What town in Oregon did you say?"

"Grants Pass. Our house is on the outskirts... in the sticks."

"That's a beautiful area. Real wooded."

"Yeah... real wooded." Her voice changed and he noticed a far away look fill her eyes.

CHAPTER 7

They sat silently gazing at the city lights in front of them, then Jeff took her hand and felt a little squeeze from hers. After a while of pointing to this light and that light saying, "Look over there. Isn't that Ventura Boulevard?" And, "See that string of car lights? That's the 405 freeway," Jeff asked if she wanted to go inside. She said that would be fine so they cozied up on the sofa with fresh glasses of wine.

The ambience could not have been more romantic with soft music and dim lighting. Jeff became brave and took her into his arms and gently kissed her lips. She, as well, felt her inhibitions melt away as her arms wrapped around his body. They embraced cautiously at first, then, giving in to their ardor, they both began seeking each other's tongues… tightening their embrace.

Jeff felt as if he would explode with passion. "Do you want to go into the bedroom?" he asked, his lips softly brushing her cheeks.

"Yes."

He guided her to his bedroom, where he lit candles that sat in stained glass holders on the dresser top and night stands. The amber glow danced off the walls and flickered warmly against the patchwork quilt on his king-sized bed. The soft music put the finishing touches on the romantic scene. She stood next to the bed waiting for him to take the lead. He approached her and slowly began removing her dress. "Are you ready for this?"

"I think so," she spoke with uncertainty. "I'm a little nervous… are you?"

"Are you kidding? I feel like a nineteenth century bride groom." He lifted her chin and smiled down at her with tenderness. "I'll go very slow. You can stop me anytime you feel uncomfortable, okay?"

"Okay."

He continued by removing her slip, then he brushed the throw pillows off the bed and pulled down the quilt and top sheet. Gently guiding her onto the bed, he quickly removed his own clothing, throwing everything onto the floor. "Are you okay?" he asked.

"Yes."

"You smell delicious."

"So do you."

He could feel her body trembling as he unsnapped her bra, taking it off and tossing it onto the pile beside the bed… and then her panties. He felt the flush of her skin against his as they started exploring each other's body's—Jeff kissing her lips… her voluptuous breasts… between her thighs.

Shawna was lost in sensations that were brand new to her. She could feel her heart beating madly in her chest.

His lips returned to hers and their excitement rose. "Do you want me?" he whispered in her ear.

"Oh yes."

His body was on top of hers. He could feel her heart pounding as he began to penetrate her slowly… as gently as he possibly could.

"Am I hurting you?" he asked.

"It's okay. It hurts, but it feels incredible."

Feeling how tight she was, he allowed her to move into him at her own pace. Soon she began pushing her pelvis into him—taking him deeper and deeper into her body. Once he had fully penetrated her, she surrendered to him completely.

Jeff's slow, deliberate movements sent her into waves of rapture. She was a spiraling fire—burning hotter and hotter. All of a sudden she let out a shriek as she exploded into a pulsating orgasm. He reached his at the same instant.

All at once, her body began thrusting into what he thought were convulsions. "Shawna! What's wrong?"

As the violent shaking continued, she began to sob hysterically. He was getting scared. "Shawna, answer me. Should I call an ambulance?"

"No…no!" she cried. "Oh God! Hold me tight, please!"

He held her as she sobbed. It was as if the floodgates had opened and she was purging something unspeakable. She kept screaming "NO!" in between wild wails of what sounded like an animal being slaughtered.

After several more bursts of tortured shrieking, her madness started to quiet down to a soft whimpering. Finally, she stopped.

Her breathing began to slow and she went limp in his arms. "What was that about?"

"I don't know," she answered, now able to take some deep breaths. "It was like I was possessed by something. Powerless to control myself. I'm so, so sorry Jeff. If I'd known something like that would happen, I wouldn't have gone through with it."

"Jesus, honey, you scared the holy shit outta me!"

Shawna lay in his arms silently as Jeff stroked her hair and pressed his cheek to hers. "Why don't you stay tonight. We can sleep in and I'll fix you breakfast."

"That sounds so nice. But, I didn't bring anything. No clothes. No toothbrush. Nothing to sleep in."

"I have a new toothbrush I haven't opened yet and you don't need anything to sleep in. We'll wear each other. I really want you to stay."

"Okay. I'll stay with you."

"I'll put a towel and the toothbrush out on the sink for you. Be right back."

It surprised Shawna that Jeff leaped from the bed bucknaked… walking around in front of her like it was nothing.

"Everything's laid out for you. I'll go after you," he instructed.

She thought, *if he isn't the least bit modest, I won't be either.* All of this was novel to her so she followed his lead, however, when she got up from the bed she gasped. "Uh oh, I got blood on your sheets." She put her hand over her mouth as innocently as a child that had unknowingly done something naughty.

"I know," he said with an understanding smile. "That's what happens the first time. Trust me, it's perfectly all right. I'll change the sheet while you're in the bathroom."

"I hope I didn't ruin it."

"I don't care."

She gave him a tender smile and walked, in her birthday suit, into the bathroom. He watched her and thought how very beautiful she was. And he was the only man ever to have made love to her—even though she had flipped out like "one possessed."

CHAPTER 8

They slept quite late on Sunday morning—awakening several times, nuzzling and smooching a little, then falling back asleep in each other's arms. Finally, at 10:00 AM, they both woke up at the same time, now with Duffy wedged in between them. "I love to sleep late," Shawna raved with a yawn and a stretch.

"Oh, a girl after my own heart. It's the best, isn't it? With all those little kids, I never once had the chance to sleep in when I was at home. I always felt sleep deprived. But I can't believe the reaction I get from my friends and family when they call and I'm still in bed at ten or eleven o'clock. And Amber was the worst. They all say, 'how can you sleep so late? You're wasting the whole day!' I keep telling them, if this is how I love to spend my off time, what's it to you? They act like I'm wasting their day. They get so upset, I'm surprised they don't call the police!"

Shawna laughed. "I get the exact same reaction. I can't figure out why people get so mad. If I wanna waste my day, it's my own business!"

"Amen to that."

She put her arms around the little dog and looked up. "Jeff, I want to apologize...."

"Don't even give it a thought. So many confusing emotions come pouring out when a woman makes love the first time." He wasn't sure that this was completely accurate, but it seemed to sooth her. He went on; "Last night was unsurpassed for me. How did… did you…?"

"It was amazing! I've never felt so wonderful in my life. Not even close."

Jeff beamed for he had wanted so much to make her first experience one she would remember… but with a glow, not with unbridled terror!

"You go ahead and shower first. I'll start breakfast." He opened a drawer and pulled out a T-shirt and a pair of his shorts. "Want to wear these so you don't have to put your dress back on?"

"Great," she said as she took the clothing with her into the bathroom.

Jeff made the bed and threw on a robe. He heard the shower running full blast. He was about to go start cooking when he saw her purse sitting on the chair—unzipped at the top. Wide open.

"I hate myself for what I'm thinking." He walked over and peered in. Her wallet was right there, unsnapped and lying open. It was as if he was a marionette and someone else was working his strings—controlling his actions. He picked it up and started looking through. *The shower's still going*, he told himself. *She'll never know.*

He leafed through credit cards and what must have been a picture of her mother. Very attractive lady. Then, he saw her driver's license. Cute picture. *Why didn't mine turn out this good? I look like the* Creature from the Black Lagoon *in mine.* Then he saw it. Her year of birth. *What?* he thought. *This doesn't add up.* He quickly did the calculations in his head. *This makes her thirty-one—a year older than me. Why would she lie about her age?*

He studied it again to see if maybe he had made a mistake. No mistake. She was thirty-one. His curiosity piqued, his hand plunged in deeper—rummaging around to see if there was anything else amiss. He moved things around until he could see everything. "Son of a bitch!" he said aloud. There, sitting at the bottom of her purse was a gun. Holding it up for inspection, he read; "Berretta-22, semi-automatic, model 950."

Just then, he heard the shower shut off. Like lightning, he placed the gun and other items back into her purse just the way he had found them. Rushing into the kitchen, he, in a wild frenzy, pulled out pans and food from the refrigerator to make it look as though he had been cooking all this time.

Thank God women take forever in the bathroom for she did not join him in the kitchen for at least fifteen minutes. By then, he had breakfast well under way. "How do you like your eggs?" he inquired.

"How about over medium?" she smiled.

"Over medium it is."

His hands were trembling as he finished cooking the meal. He served it out on the patio where they could enjoy the spectacular, daytime view.

As they ate, Shawna kept looking at him with affection. Jeff kept his gaze fixed on the view, but could feel her eyes penetrating him. He tried to keep the conversation light; however, she seemed to be in the mood for intimate words.

"Jeff, there's no way you could possibly know what you gave to me last night. You were so sweet and caring. It… it was beyond wonderful."

He turned to her and let out a big sigh, "You blew my mind, Shawna. You were so soft and innocent." He hesitated for a moment, then, "Why do I feel like there's so much I don't know about you?"

She gave him a warm smile. "I guess it takes time to feel like we really know each other. I want to know you on a deep level. It's probably too soon to be saying this, but I've never known any man with the depth that I see in you."

Then, why are you lying to me? he thought, but said nothing.

CHAPTER 9

"Dinner—7PM—Pedro's—My treat—Gotta talk!" was the message on Kevin's pager.

"So what's the emergency?" Kevin asked as he slid into the booth and sat down across from his buddy.

"Hey, first, what happened to your face?"

"Why, what do you mean?" Kevin sheepishly responded.

"I don't know, something's different. I could tell right away." Jeff was studying Kevin's face—trying to figure out what the change was.

"Well, I'm seeing this new chick, Tiffany, and she tinted my eyebrows and eyelashes. She just got her esthetician's license and she wanted to practice. It's no big deal."

Jeff just couldn't let this one go by. Unable to stifle his amusement, he watched his buddy, now self-conscious, frantically trying to rub the darkness off his brows. "She said nobody would notice—that it would bring out my beautiful, green eyes."

"I don't know..." Jeff said, still pondering the new look. "I think I liked you better all washed out."

"It'll wear off in about three weeks."

"Good."

"I'm taking her to see that new movie that came out, "King Kong meets Godzilla". So which one do you think Jeff?"

Jeff pondered this for a moment. "Well, King Kong is a great ape—Godzilla's a lizard." Kevin held up a strong fist, "KONG it is!"

"So, what's this big thing you have to tell me?" Kevin demanded.

"She stayed over last Saturday night."

"No shit! Well?" He shifted forward in his seat.

"She was definitely a virgin."

"Wow! How was it? This is probably the closest I'll ever be to knowing."

"I don't know why I tell you these things. You're such a superficial moron. It was great, if you must know. She was amazing. But after we finished, she had a complete meltdown. I thought she was having some kind of attack. I kid you not. I almost called 911."

"Get outta town! What happened?"

"She just started shaking and sobbing... and screaming."

"What was she screaming?"

"Oh, stuff like; 'No, no! Get away! Stop!' I don't know what else. I couldn't understand her."

"Shit! What did you do?"

"I just held her until she quieted down. Then she was fine. I mean she was back to normal. But wait, it gets better...or worse."

"You are a wealth of entertainment. Please go on."

"When she was in the shower, I noticed that her purse was open. I couldn't stop myself, Kev. I pulled out her driver's license and low and behold, she's not twenty-five. She's thirty-one!"

"Get out!"

"But it gets even more bizarre. I found a gun on the bottom of her purse. A goddamned gun!"

"I was on to her from the get! But what's even weirder is now she's a THIRTY-ONE-year-old virgin!"

"Will you stop with that? Don't you think I should be more worried about the fucking gun?"

Kevin leaned over the table as a weighty expression fell across his face. Jeff leaned in close, in eager anticipation of some profound advice.

"My friend, I would like you to know that Shawna is

completely safe. YOU'RE in danger, but she's completely safe."

Jeff threw his hands up; "Why do I ever think I can confide anything serious to you?"

Kevin stuck out his bottom lip into a pout. Then he spoke in a more somber tone; "I don't know—a lot of women carry guns in their purses. Maybe she was attacked or something—or maybe she's an undercover cop or a secret agent. If she was gonna shoot you, she would've done it by now, right?"

Jeff shook his head at all of his buddy's imaginative explanations, "I've never known any woman who packed a rod. You wouldn't find that a bit unnerving?"

"Not nearly as much as being a thirty-one-year-old virgin!"

"Will you get off that?"

"Well, are you gonna ask her why she lied to you?"

"I can't. Then she'll know I went snooping through her purse"

"Are you just gonna let this go? I told you she was trouble, Jeffrey. Has she got her hooks in you already?"

"There's some explanation for why she lied. I can just sense the good in her. I'm not kidding. Kev, I really feel something. What am I gonna do?"

"Rip up her phone number and forget you ever met her."

"I know you're right… but…."

"You're hopeless. When are you gonna see her again?"

"I don't know. She went home to Oregon to see her mother. She's dying of cancer."

"No kidding. Does she have any other family?"

"Just a younger brother. Seventeen… she says."

Just then, the waitress came to take their order. "I'll have lobster tails," Kevin stated emphatically.

The waitress did not look amused. "This is a Mexican restaurant. We don't have lobster tails."

"But my buddy's buying."

"How about lobster enchiladas?" she offered.

"Is that expensive?"

The waitress just glared at him, obviously becoming more annoyed by the minute.

"He'll have lobster enchiladas!" Jeff ordered for him. "And I'll have a chicken tostada… grande."

"So, you're seeing some new girl now? The esthetician?" Jeff asked. "Where'd you meet this one?"

"At Dillon's."

"Dildos?"

"Dillon's, you idiot—that happening place that opened up in Westwood."

"Isn't that a pick up joint? A meat market?" Jeff ribbed.

"It's an upscale nightclub with live bands on two floors… dancing… you can get dinner there if you want—steaks and everything."

"A meat market," he repeated. " Haven't you seen Joyce again?"

"Emily, you bird-brain. No, it just wasn't happening with her. We had absolutely nothing in common."

"She dumped ya, huh?"

"Yeah."

CHAPTER 10

Jeff was wrapping up his action figure prototype when Ginny buzzed him. "You have a call on line two," she said with a hint of teasing in her voice.

It had been three weeks and he had not called Shawna. His brain and his emotions were engaged in a full-blown tug-of-war now. He was more attracted to her than any woman he had ever known. He had felt nothing even close to this when he met Amber. On one hand, he was head over heels… on the other hand, Kevin was right, there was something strange going on with her.

With the way Ginny was talking, he had a feeling that this was Shawna on the line. He certainly didn't want her to think he was giving her the brush after their first night together.

"This is Jeffrey Daniels."

"Hi, Jeffrey Daniels. Remember me?"

"Oh Shawna! It's so good to hear your voice. I was just going to call you. How was your trip and your mother?"

"The cancer's spread. She won't be going home again. They're gonna put her in a convalescent home. She's dying, Jeff," she said as she broke into tears.

"Oh honey, I am sorry. This is the second parent you've lost—and you're so young. What can I do to help you?"

"May I see you tonight?" she asked.

"Absolutely. How about dinner? Somewhere quiet where we can talk."

"That'd be wonderful."

"Pick you up at seven. We'll go to Jason's. I miss you, Shawna."

"Do you? I miss you too... big-time."

I can't confront her with the lie about her age and the gun now, when she just found out she's losing her mother, Jeff thought on the way to pick up Shawna. I'll have to say something eventually... but not tonight.

When she opened her door, she looked ravishing. Jeff had a good mind to suggest skipping dinner, but he knew this would not be good etiquette. She invited him in while she grabbed her jacket from the coat rack as the weather had just started turning a bit chilly.

Jason's was a lovely restaurant with private booths and soft, candlelight. They enjoyed a delicious and peaceful dinner. To Jeff's delight, the conversation flowed pretty easily. They spoke, in depth, about her mother and how Shawna was dealing with this tragic news. They talked more about Jeff's family and he invited her for Thanksgiving dinner. "That is, if you can stand the commotion—and some of them have their own kids now. A lot of 'em!"

Shawna eagerly accepted his offer. "I can't wait to meet them," she told him. "Being with you has made me feel so much better tonight. I was so low before. When my mother goes, I won't have anyone."

"What about your brother?"

"Yes. I do have him," she replied through misty eyes.

Jeff thought that was another odd thing to say. Perhaps they were not close.

After dinner, he drove Shawna home and she asked him to come in for a drink. As soon as she closed her door, his arms were around her and they melted into a deep, passionate kiss. "Will you stay over with me tonight?" she asked.

"Yes! Oh yes!"

The next Saturday, Jeff met Kevin for golf at one of their favorite courses. As they were sitting in the cart at the first tee, Jeff blurted out, "It's no use—she's got me hooked. I don't care if she lies and shoots people—I'm falling in love with her."

"What if she's the black widow? Gets guys to marry her, then kills 'em for their money?"

"Then she wouldn't have been a virgin, doofus."

"Oh yeah. Well, sleep with one eye open. What if she sneaks up in the middle of the night and blows your fucking…."

"Will you stop? Now, I'm gonna be nervous to shut my eyes when I'm with her. You know, we're blowing this gun thing way out of proportion. If I asked her, she'd probably say, 'oh yeah, I carry it for protection when I'm driving alone at night. No biggie.'"

"Then why don't you ask her?" Kevin said with a smirk on his face.

"I will… when the time is right. Maybe it'll come up on it's own."

"I'll bet not."

In an attempt to divert the topic of conversation, Jeff asked how it was going with Tiffany… the esthetician.

"Funny you should ask that. Tiffany's old news—no substance. But I met this nurse who works at one of the doctor's offices on my route. Usually, the receptionist signs in the samples, but this drop dead gorgeous nurse did it this time. Her name's April. I'd never seen her there before so I had to work fast. I asked her out for dinner and she said yes. That quick."

"Did you go out yet?"

"Yeah. It was great! Actually, we met at Pedro's for dinner. We're going out again next weekend. How about that?"

Jeff nodded. "It doesn't surprise me. There's not a shy bone in your body."

CHAPTER 11

When Thanksgiving arrived, Jeff was full of doubts about exposing Shawna to his insane family. But she had to meet them sooner or later. He had apprised her of the wild kids and of his elderly grandparents; Hector and Agnes who lived a mere two blocks away but always drove over. "Hector's a hypochondriac," he told her. "He'll share everything about his bodily functions. And they both gripe and grumble about everything. The way the world has gone to the dogs. How things were real different when they grew up. All that stuff."

She simply nodded, "I don't mind that a bit, Jeff."

The two of them had plane tickets to fly to Oregon after the holiday. Shawna wanted Jeff to meet her mother before she passed away. A horrible way to put it, but a fact nevertheless. She was going to put the house up for sale, so Jeff offered to help her pack everything up while he was there. Then, they would call the real estate agent and put it on the market.

"Where's your brother gonna live?"

Her eyes became disdainful. "I'll be forced to bring him down here to live with me until he's older."

"How much older?" Jeff asked trying to hide his disappointment.

"Until he gets some kind of a job. He can't support himself now."

"He's planning on college, isn't he?"

"I don't think so."

How could a young man almost out of high school not be planning to go on to college? he wondered. What kind of future could he make for himself? And it did not escape his notice that each time Shawna spoke of her brother, an odd expression came over her face. Maybe he was retarded or handicapped. But why wouldn't she just tell him if this were the case.

They pulled up to the two-story house where Jeff grew up. It was located in a middle-class neighborhood in Van Nuys. Shawna thought it could be very cute with a little more attention. The front yard hosted an enormous deciduous tree that appeared to have been neglected since the beginning of its numerous years. The fall breezes aided in the sprinkling of dead leaves that were now scattered over the entire lawn. The ones that chose to fall onto the roof were quickly blown off to thicken the blanket over the front yard grass. The house itself was in dire need of a paint job showing worn spots on the tan stucco, and the russet-colored trim was crusting with age. It was difficult to picture Jeff growing up here. His house was as perfect as this one was imperfect.

"One thing my dad was right about was when I was looking to buy a house," Jeff said, pointing to the lawn. "He told me, 'If it has a deciduous tree on the property, run like hell in the other direction.' As quick as you rake these damn leaves up, it's back the same way an hour later."

"My house was basically in the woods so no one seemed to care much about leaves in their yards," she told him.

They knocked and the door swung open. There stood a boy of about four years of age, one hand on the doorknob and the other holding one of those big, round suckers. It appeared that a good portion of it had somehow ended up all over his hands, face and now the doorknob.

Jeff bent over with a smile, "May we come in, Joey?" Joey said nothing and slammed the door in their faces. "See what I mean?"

Shawna could not contain her laughter. Jeff pushed the doorbell about ten times in a row. Maybe someone a little older would hear it over all the screaming, crying and noisy conversation.

This time, another little boy opened the door. He took one look at the couple and tore off in the other direction to where his mother was engaged in conversation with other family members. "They're here! They're here!" he shrieked… then, "Who are those people?"

"It's your uncle Jeff and his girlfriend!" his mom embarrassedly informed him. "Jeff! Come in. And you must be Shawna. We're all under the strictest orders to be on our best behavior today."

"This is Betsy, one of my sisters," Jeff introduced, shaking his head.

The two women shook hands, then Jeff and Shawna entered the madhouse. "Oh my God." Shawna was bowled over by the sound level and the sheer number of people crowded into the downstairs rooms of the house. Her eyes scanned the rooms as she beheld the inside of Jeff's childhood residence.

Although the carpet was stained and the furniture was worse for the wear, there was definitely an aura of warmth and love in the air. There were children running up and down the stairs, groups of people talking, kids diving off furniture, babies wailing, what seemed like wives shouting orders to their husbands and there was an older, white-haired couple sitting on the sofa, each with a kid in their lap. She thought they must be the infamous grandparents.

"This is unbelievable!" Shawna said, dropping her jaw.

"I warned you."

They made their way through the mob, Jeff introducing

as they moved along; this is Wesley, this is Shirley, Amy, Jack, Brian, Barbara, Dennis, Melissa, Paul etc.... Finally, they came to a middle-aged couple standing next to the fireplace talking with another group of adults. "Shawna, this is my mom, Debbie and my dad, Ray." Shawna held out her hand and shot an ear-to-ear grin toward the friendly-looking couple.

"How nice to finally meet both of you," she said.

"Jeff stays away as much as possible. We can only get him here on major holidays. We've sure been looking forward to meeting you," Ray said. "You were right Jeff, she's positively hot!"

"Dad!" A red-faced Jeff looked over to see Shawna in hysterics. "I'm glad you think he's funny."

They made the rounds to meet as many family members as possible. There were husbands and wives of his siblings, nieces and nephews, aunts and uncles. Finally, they sat down to dinner. There were tables set up in the living room, the den, the kitchen, the patio, but they sat Jeff and Shawna at the dining room table with his parents, grandparents, Hector and Agnes and some of his sisters and brothers.

There were a lot of women serving platters of turkey, stuffing, green beans and mashed potatoes and gravy to each guest. Shawna thought these must be his sisters doing the serving. She figured they must have cooked at least five large turkeys to serve this crowd. After a time, everyone was seated and they dove into the scrumptious meal.

At the table, they all engaged in small talk, asking where Shawna worked and how she and Jeff had met. She told the crazy story of how she had dumped her drink all over him. Everyone roared with laughter knowing just how meticulous Jeff was about his appearance.

Jeff's grandfather, Hector, started right in with his typical ranting about which she had been forewarned. Debbie had asked Shawna if she did most of her work on computer. Just as she opened her mouth to answer, Hector bluntly broke in, "There were no computers when I was growin' up and we got along just fine. Those dadgum contraptions…who the hell can figure 'em out? They got 'em in every damn thing we use—even the cars. I've had my car for three years and I still can't work the radio or the heat or the defogger. And now, they've found a way to charge for everything you use. This crazy cable TV. TV was free when I was young. A little box with a black an' white picture." He let out a gut laugh as his palm slammed down hard on the tabletop.

"The picture would start rollin'. Back then, you had to get up and walk across the room to adjust it. Then as quick as you sat your butt back down, it would start rollin' the other way…"

"But Dad," Debbie interrupted. "We have so much to be grateful for nowadays—all the modern conveniences. So many things to make our lives easier."

"You kids've got a lot to be thankful for," he said, pointing his finger at Jeff and Shawna. "Got your whole lives in front of you. So much to do. So much to experience. Got your health. When you get to be my age, you'll be thankful for a good bowel movement!"

"Hector! Are you crazy talking about that at the dinner table?" Jeff shouted. "I'm sorry," he told Shawna shaking his head. She was laughing so hard, she almost choked on her turkey.

"Jeff's always been the touchy one," his grandfather went on. "You know, persnickety about noise and every little thing bein' in its place. Like an old maid in britches, this boy." The old man gave in to a good belly laugh—clearly amused with himself. "I don't see how he survived this madhouse growin' up. But lemme tell ya, he sure hightailed it outta here, hell bent for leather the minute he was old enough. Wanted to go to a college as far from the homestead as he could git!"

"Hector, Shawna doesn't wanna hear stories about how…"

"Yes, I do!" she interrupted.

"Jeff never did have much patience with children," his mother, Debbie, added. "He used to bribe the kids to go to sleep early. Money for the older ones—candy for the little ones. It's the only way he could get time for his studies, sharing a room with two younger bothers an' all. He always got top grades, though. We were real proud of him for that."

"So Dad, I see the old tree is still creating a major mess in the yard," Jeff interrupted, attempting to steer the dinner table talk to a more impersonal subject. "Do the gardeners still come to…"

"Those yardmen with their damn blowers!" Hector chimed in. "The stepping stones in my back yard used to be flush with the ground—now they stick up a good three inches from the dirt. I told those guys, 'you've blown half my yard down the street! I used to have eleven thousand square feet—now I've got ten thousand!'"

It was no use trying to start any kind of conversation—not with Hector spouting his mouth off at everything you said. Jeff just sat back and kept quiet while Hector droned on and on about every last thing that was wrong with every last thing.

As people finished their dinners, they began getting up from their tables and mixing with the crowd. Shawna could not help noticing that the whole house looked like a cyclone had just blown through. There was food all over the floor, drinks spilled on tabletops and on carpet, utensils on the floor. Broken glass was scattered all over the kitchen tile. Diapers were dirty. Babies were crying. Children were again, running, jumping, screaming, hitting, tattling on one another.

So this was the environment in which Jeff had grown up. This explained a lot about his perfect, immaculate home, his fastidious personal hygiene, his eternal pursuit for peace and quiet—and most of all, his adamant decision not to have children.

"Jeff, can you direct me to the lady's room?" Shawna asked after a few more introductions to family members.

"Straight down that hall, second door on your left."

"Thanks, don't go far. I might get lost in the crowd."

"I'll be right here."

But when she walked into the bathroom, there were two little boys playing in the toilet. They had a tugboat and a sailboat floating around in the commode. "Excuse me, boys," she said, but they did not look up. She would have let it go; however, her need to pee was imminent.

She found Jeff again. "There are two little boys playing in the toilet. I couldn't get their attention."

"Jesus Christ!" he shouted, stomping into the bathroom. "Todd! Mathew! Get the hell out of there. Janice, come and get your monsters!"

Janice came running. "Jeff, you don't have to… hey! Get outta there, right now! I oughta blister your bottoms!" she yelled as she grabbed the pair by their shirts. When the coast was clear, Jeff apologized profusely to Shawna who was about to wet her pants from laughing along with her urgent need to use the facilities.

"Jeff," she said, tapping his shoulder. "The boats are still in there."

"What boats?" He peered into the john. "Oh shit!" He pulled the toys out with his bare hands and quickly wiped the seat with a hand towel. "I'm so sorry, honey," he cried as he stepped out, closing the door behind him. He heard the lock snap, then he walked back to the living room to read Janice the riot act.

After pumpkin pie with whipped cream was served, Jeff told everyone that they had to leave as they had an early flight for Oregon the next morning. "Please bring Jeff back to see us sooner than next year, Shawna. We loved having you. You're always welcome in our home."

"Thank you. It was nice meeting all of you. I had a wonderful time. Bye," Shawna shouted as she waved to the group. It tickled her to see at least twelve little kids waving good-bye to her. They had no idea who she was, but they were enthusiastically waving and shouting goodbyes.

Jeff pulled out from the curb and drove a few blocks away,

then pulled over to the side of the street. He shoved the car into park and buried his face in both hands.

"What's wrong?" she pleaded. He looked over at her with disbelief in his eyes.

"I ruined your Thanksgiving, taking you there. I should have known better. What a disaster. Now, you see what I mean about my family. I wasn't exaggerating, was I?"

"Oh Jeff," she laughed. "You take all of that so seriously. I had so much fun. I really did! Your family is wonderful… and your grandfather's a riot."

"You're so special," he said. "No one else would have been so understanding." He leaned over and placed his hands on either side of her face. "I washed my hands," he informed. She laughed, then their lips met as they melted into a deep kiss. When they released their embrace, he looked deeply into her eyes. "I love you," he said.

"I love you, too."

CHAPTER 12

The next morning, they loaded their bags into the trunk of Jeff's car and drove to LAX. He had spent the night with Shawna at her apartment since it was closer to the airport. They checked their bags at the counter and were issued their boarding passes. "May I see each one of your I.D.'s?" the clerk asked. Instantly, Jeff thought, this is my golden opportunity. I can't blow this.

She reached into her wallet and pulled out her driver's license. She tried to hold on to it as she held it up for the clerk to view; however, he took it from her and inspected it carefully. "Thank you," he said as he handed it back, but just as she was taking it, Jeff snatched it out of her hand.

"Hey, that's a great picture! Look how bad mine turned out," he said as he showed her his license that the clerk had just given back. She made a mad attempt to grab her license away from him, but he had a firm hold on it—studying it carefully as they stepped away from the counter.

"Honey... is this right? Your date of birth? You said you were twenty-five."

She gave up trying to yank it out of his hand. Her secret was out. He knew.

"Well... I was embarrassed to tell you how old I really am. Thirty-one and never had a boyfriend. I was afraid you'd think there was something wrong with me. When you asked how old

I was, 'twenty-five' just came flying out of my mouth. Can you forgive me?"

"You never need to lie or hide anything from me, Shawna. I want you to tell me everything about you. How else can we ever grow close? I would have found out eventually anyway. Please don't ever think you have to keep anything from me." He lifted her chin and looked solidly into her eyes. "Okay?"

"Okay."

Now, if another golden opportunity would present itself to explain the gun, all would be out in the open. No more secrets.

The plane trip was not a pleasant one for Jeff as there was a baby two rows up engaging in earsplitting shrieks that echoed throughout the entire cabin. This time, he could not throw down twenty dollars and walk out.

And if that were not bad enough, a little boy of about five was engaging in one screaming tantrum after another. He was using the aisle for a runway pretending to take off like a plane. Up and down and up and down, with the added bonus of his stentorian sound effects of a jet engine. The flight attendant repeatedly spoke to the parents informing them they needed to restrain their son—they could not have him running about the cabin in this manner. But each time the parents tried to get little Sidney to sit down in his seat, new roars of protest went ripping through the plane. "NO! NO! Lemme alone. Lemme do what I wanna do!"

Both parents were completely impotent in controlling their little hellion. No sooner had they put him in his seat, and he was up again. By the end of the flight, everyone on board knew his name: "Sidney, sit down! Sidney, be quiet! Sidney, I'm going to count to ten! Sidney, stop, Sidney don't! SIDNEY! SIDNEY! SIDNEY!" His tantrums and airplane imitations along with the infant's, two rows up, continuous shrieking made for the hellhole of Jeff's worst nightmares.

As he sat trying desperately to find a way to endure this bedlam, his attention was snagged by a woman seated across the aisle from him… a woman who looked like she had swallowed a beach ball—like the baby should have been born three weeks ago. Jeff was thoroughly amused by the horror-struck looks she and her husband kept flashing to each other as they too were forced to endure the commotion of the two little ones. "Must be her first," he whispered in Shawna's ear. Then, leaning over as far as he could, he addressed himself to the expectant mother, "Keep it on the inside as long as you can!" He spoke in a loud, clear voice—plainly meant to be heard by everyone. The entire cabin howled with laughter.

Everything else went pretty smoothly. They landed at the Medford Airport, picked up their luggage and rented a car. Shawna had suggested that they have Jared pick them up in her mother's car, but Jeff had a "thing" about imposing on people and driving someone else's car. This was better, he had told her. Then they would have their own car when they needed it. Jared might need his mother's car for a date or something. Shawna gave him a puzzled look.

They drove straight to the convalescent home to see Mrs. Reese. "She's in room twenty-seven," the woman at the front desk informed. Jeff followed Shawna through the door. After peeking into the first bed, she continued on to the other bed next to the window. Jeff was shocked at the emaciated appearance of the woman in front of him. She was a skeleton with sunken cheeks and black circles around her eyes. Her skin was thin and yellow—sagging from the bone. Jeff thought she must be dead. No person could look this ghastly and still be alive. But when Shawna leaned over and kissed her forehead, she opened her eyes and smiled. "My baby's here," she said. Shawna kissed her again.

"I'm here, Mom. I'm gonna stay with you as much as I can for the next few days. I brought someone, Mom. This is Jeff."

"I'm so glad to meet you, Mrs. Reese," he said as he lifted her frail hand from her side.

"Call me Ellen," she spoke in a voice so weak, he had to put his ear close to her face. "Are you Shawna's boyfriend?"

Jeff met Shawna's eyes and they exchanged a tender smile. "Yes, I am."

"Oh, I'm so happy for the two of you. She hasn't dated much, you know. I'm so glad she has you now." She looked up at her daughter. "Honey, you finally let someone in. You don't know how I've prayed every day that you would meet a nice man. My baby… I can stop worrying. I can rest now. At last, you found love."

Jeff thought her words a bit strange, but she seemed so sweet, so motherly. Probably, she was just a concerned mom. Wanted to see her daughter happy before she exited this world.

Ellen wanted to talk to Shawna about something so Jeff stepped out into the hall to give them some time alone.

"Shawna."

"Yes, Mom?"

"Please watch over Jared. He has problems, you know."

"I know, Mom. Has anything happened? Is there something I should know?"

"A few months ago, when I was still home, I caught him peeping in Jenny Kirkpatrick's window. No one else saw him. He promised never to do it again. Said it was the first time. I don't know." Ellen shook her head ever so slightly.

"Oh God!" she blurted, then quickly regretted her knee jerk reaction to her little brother's foul behavior. "Well, don't you worry one bit, Mom. I'm going to take him to live with me in Los Angeles. I'll watch over him. Please don't worry. I love you so much."

"I love you too, my little pumpkin. It's just that, I don't have long and I need to know everything's in order. You're selling the house, right?"

"Yes. Jeff came to help me with the packing and the sale... and most of all to meet you. I'm so glad you got to meet him. You were right, Mom. There was a nice man out there for me. I really love him. He's a good person."

Her mother smiled with as much enthusiasm as she could muster. Shawna asked Jeff to come back in to say goodnight. They both kissed her and said they would return the next afternoon.

It was only 3PM so they thought they would be able to get a good start on getting things packed up. Shawna had had boxes delivered by a moving company so they would be able to get right to work.

Following Shawna's directions, they soon drove up to a small, one-story house that was pretty much out in the sticks. It was a wooded area with a few homes scattered here and there. The blue, stucco house was in a state of disrepair with paint peeling off the dingy, white trim, screens torn and the grass in the front yard hadn't been mowed in so long, it had gone to seed.

"So, this is where you grew up?" he asked.

"My whole life, until I went off to college. Then, I really wanted to settle in L.A. I'd planned on it for years. Sorry about the condition of the house. My mom hasn't been able to keep it up since she's been so sick."

"Oh, don't apologize. I totally understand. You saw my family's house," he said, but he silently wondered why a healthy seventeen-year-old was not doing this work.

"Come on in, Jeff," she said as she opened the door with her key.

He stepped in to see a very modest home. The inside, as well, looked as though it hadn't been painted in twenty years. The walls were a discolored white and the curtains were old and dingy. The furniture was pedestrian; a beige davenport and overstuffed chair, walnut veneered coffee table and end tables. Lamps that looked like they were bought from a thrift store—all unmatched, all with torn and stained shades. The thought struck him how similar the houses they had grown up were and how both of them had turned out to be so exceedingly meticulous with their own homes.

"It's nothing like your showplace, is it?" Shawna looked embarrassed.

"All I care about is that this is where you grew up—where you spent your life. I want to know everything about your life, Shawna."

"I'll show you around. This is the living room," she joked. "And you take a half turn to the right and you're in the kitchen," she said as they walked into a small, shabby room with outdated appliances and a small, red kitchen table with matching chairs that now had brown stuffing escaping from the rips and tears in the plastic upholstery.

She showed him her mother's bedroom—a tiny room with a double bed taking up most of the space. An old dresser and a metal file cabinet wedged into the corner. Then, Shawna opened the door to her bedroom. A single bed with a pink lace bed cover and a menagerie of stuffed animals strategically placed over the entire surface, a maple dresser with cosmetics, photos and candles on top, a bench placed at the foot of the bed and pink, lace curtains on the two windows. There was no carpeting in this room. They were standing on very worn, hardwood floors that creaked with each shift of their weight.

"So this is your little girl room?" Jeff asked.

"It's real different from my apartment in L.A., isn't it?"

"It tells me a lot about you. It's so girlie," he chuckled as he picked up a photo from the dresser top. "This you?" he asked.

"Yeah, that's when I was five years old—just before I started kindergarten."

"Twenty-six years ago, huh?" he jeered, looking up to catch her reaction.

"Yeah," she laughed. "Twenty-six years ago."

Shawna showed him the one bathroom—a small, white

room with a toilet, a sink set into a tile surface with cabinets underneath and a tub that sat on four feet with a showerhead extending from the wall. Then they walked back through the hallway, passing a closed door on the left.

"And is this Jared's room?' Jeff asked.

She nodded., "He'll come out when he's ready."

"He's home?"

Shawna nodded. "I think so. The car's in the driveway."

What in the world was this all about? He was in his room, but didn't come out to greet his own sister or meet her new boyfriend? He had a weird feeling that really bothered him because he now wanted everything to be smooth going between Shawna and him. Why couldn't he shake this eerie suspicion that he was getting himself deeper and deeper involved with something he could not handle.

"Well, let's get to work on packing, shall we?" she said.

"Bring on the boxes!" he replied. "How about I start on the kitchen?"

"I'll get the boxes from the garage."

Shawna went out and came back with armfuls of boxes. Jeff dug into the kitchen drawers and Shawna went to work in her own room. After about an hour, that door in the hallway creaked opened and the seventeen-year-old brother stepped out.

Jeff was absorbed in his job of pulling out pans from the lower cabinets and carefully packing them into boxes. He sealed each one with tape, then labeled it; "kitchen / pans." Something caused him to look up and when he did, he was unable to stifle a horrified gasp—a gasp that caused his whole body to jerk. A spine-chilling silence filled the room as Jeff tried to snap himself back to reality.

His mind tried to assimilate the six-foot figure standing in the doorway, looking down at him. He thought it was the most nefarious face he had ever beheld. The hair was dark—almost black and it hung in greasy strings that plastered against his pasty, white forehead. His skin was covered with oozing; acne pustules and his frontal bone protruded into a heavy ridge over his eyes, giving him a dark, sinister appearance. He had a few days growth of shadowy whiskers, which only added to his malevolent aura.

Jeff tried to hide his shock as he stood and extended his hand. "You must be Jared. Hi, I'm Jeff." Jared's eyes were cast down as he held out his hand. Jeff almost recoiled from the weak, wet noodle feel of Jared's hand. Limp handshakes from men were one of his pet peeves.

The boy said nothing so Jeff attempted to make small talk. "Your sinister's packing up boxes in her room. I mean, your sister." He felt a ripple of mortification pulsate through his body at his blunder in speech. "I came with her from Los Angeles to lend a hand. I hope I can be of some help."

"I'll take care of my room. I don't need any help in there." He spoke in a deep monotone, completely devoid of any expression. And as he spoke, Jeff caught flashes of his teeth—or what once were teeth. Crooked, brown things that looked as if everything he had ever eaten had taken up permanent residence between them. Old stuff, maybe food particles cemented in solidly with thick, crusted tarter. Hadn't he ever heard of dental floss? Jeff wondered. But how the hell could he get a piece of floss between those things? They all ran together like one continuous, disgusting entity.

"Whatever you say, Jared," he said, inching back against the cabinet before he got a whiff of what this guy's breath must smell like. "We'll let you take care of your own stuff. I'll just stay with the kitchen and living room. Plenty to do right here. Are you looking forward to living in LA?"

"I guess."

Just then, Shawna came out of her room and walked up behind Jared. "Oh, I see you've met my brother."

How the hell could this thing be Shawna's brother? She was so soft…so sweet…so pretty. This guy had the personality of a corps. In fact, he looked like he'd been dead for at least three weeks—no, make that three months. Jeff saw no family resemblance whatsoever.

"Yes, we introduced ourselves." Jeff said as he started on the dishes in the cupboard above the sink. He tried to look busy so that Shawna would not see the disbelief in his eyes.

It was five o'clock and dark outside. Shawna offered, "How about if I call and order a pizza? There's nothing in the house to fix and that'll be easy."

"Sounds wonderful," Jeff said as he kept his face buried into his task.

"Jared? Okay?" she asked.

"Yeah, fine."

Jared reached into his pocket and pulled out a pack of cigarettes and a small plastic lighter. He shook one cigarette out and lit up. Jeff immediately started swatting at the air.

"Jared, go outside if you're gonna smoke that," his sister ordered.

"It's freezing out there," he protested.

"Either that or put it out."

He groaned and walked out the back door. "So that's your brother," Jeff said still attempting to digest the scene.

"Pretty scary, huh? Now you know why he wouldn't be needing the car to go on any dates."

Jeff gave her a forced smile, but he was far from feeling light hearted. "How old was he when he started smoking?" he asked.

"I don't know—three, I think."

When the pizza came, Jared grabbed two large pieces and disappeared into his room again.

"What does he do in there for all these hours?" Jeff inquired.

"He's on the computer most of the time. Other than that, I don't ask him."

"Has he always been like this... I mean... so withdrawn... so..."

"Hideous?" she snickered. "He's always been an outcast. Keeps to himself—never had any friends. Mom and dad tried over and over to get help for him, but nothing worked. They took him to medical clinics to see if he had some chemical imbalance or something. Took him to years of therapy. I'm so afraid he'll always be a recluse. Mom worries that he'll never be able to hold any kind of job the way he is."

"Well, maybe he'll outgrow this stage. You know how teenagers are. You can't pull two words out of them. And getting them to wash their face or brush their teeth can be a pipe dream."

"I don't know, Jeff. He's not normal." No shit! Jeff thought to himself. Shawna went on, "He's never been any different. I hate to say this, but I don't want to be stuck with him for the rest of my life."

"I know what you mean. It's an unusual situation. He's not retarded, at least not mentally. It just doesn't seem fair that you have to be responsible for your parents' child. You certainly didn't ask for this responsibility."

"It was so easy when my mom could look after him. They could have stayed here in the house and everything would have been fine. But now that she's dying, I'm the only family member left. What can I do?"

Jeff just shook his head. "Does he go to school?"

"No. He refused to go back two years ago. He said he hates all those weirdoes. When he was in the second grade, the kids nicknamed him "Zombie" and it stuck right on through junior high till he dropped out after the tenth grade. The other kids never warmed up to him. He was an outcast the whole time."

"Zombie, huh?" Jeff said. He thought, I've never heard a more apt nickname.

"Supposedly, he was being home schooled," Shawna continued. "But Mom gave up on that. She could never get him to sit down and pay attention."

"Are you gonna put him in school when he gets to L.A?"

"He won't go. I can enroll him, but I know he'll refuse to show up."

"God Shawna, I didn't realize what a terrible predicament you were in."

Shawna's eyes began to sting as tears started to spill down her cheeks. Jeff took her in his arms and rocked her tenderly. He did not want to say anything to her, but her brother scared the bejesus out of him. It was almost as if there was an evil energy oozing from the kid and Jeff desperately wanted to get the hell out of there. There was a dark force in the air—it was unmistakable.

CHAPTER 13

Ellen's bed was stacked high with packed boxes so Shawna asked Jeff if he wanted to sleep on the davenport in the living room, or if he would like to share her bed with her. The only thing was that it was a very small, single bed and they would have to sleep squished together all night. She did not know if he would be comfortable. He instantly took her up on her offer to share her bed. He wasn't about to stay out in the living room with his eyes closed all night. Not with "Frankenstein" hanging out in the next room.

They woke early the next morning—both of them stiff and sore from the cramped sleeping arrangements. Jeff had had some romantic fantasies about making love with her in the home—the room she grew up in, however; circumstances were turning out to be anything but romantic.

They took turns showering and using the bathroom. There was no sign of "The Creeper." Shawna knocked on his door to see if he wanted to go to breakfast with them, but there was no answer. She opened the door a crack, but the room was empty. She looked out to see that her mother's car was gone from the driveway.

"He must have gone out somewhere. He'll probably get breakfast at McDonald's."

She and Jeff went to a little, country style diner for breakfast then headed right back to resume their packing project. Jared was home when they arrived.

It was the same thing as the previous night with Jared either answering their questions with a one or two word response or not at all. One thing Jeff noticed was that with any type of interaction, Jared kept his eyes cast down. He would never look anyone directly in the face.

In the afternoon, Shawna suggested that she and Jared go to visit their mother. Jeff told her he would keep working on the packing while they were gone. He was really making some headway and he wanted to give the two of them some private time with Ellen.

They left for the convalescent home as Jeff was finishing the living room. He would tackle the bathroom next. After working for about an hour, he could not blot out the thought of just taking a peek in Jared's room. Why had he been so adamant about no one helping him in there?

"I'm sorry, God, but you'd be curious too." He unlatched the door and pushed it open—enough to see that the room was in complete disarray. He stepped in and was hit with a stale, repulsive odor. "Jesus Christ, what a craphole!" he said out loud. Didn't this kid ever bathe? Or clean his room? And he's going to come live with Shawna in her immaculate apartment.

It was as if some force had taken over his body and he was powerless to fight against it. He began rummaging through stacks of CD's, newspapers, computer printouts, magazines. The pile of magazines grabbed his attention. He started leafing through the pages of porno magazines—not girlie magazines, but hard-core porn. Jeff had never seen anything like this in his entire life. Women and men in bondage, young girls being whipped, brutalized and gang raped. Naked women tied up with bruises and cuts and cigarette burns all over their bodies. "Oh my God," he exclaimed. "This kid is not shy—he's sick... extremely sick."

He threw down the stack of magazines and opened a cabinet under the TV stand. It was filled with videos that appeared to be even worse than the reading material. Hard-core porn and something Jared had labeled "snuff films." *What the hell could that be?*

Could Shawna and the mother possibly not know this was going on under their own roof? This kid's fascination with sexual violence? The room certainly looked and smelled as though no one had come in to clean in at least ten years. But didn't Ellen worry that her son was troubled? Of course, she had been sick for the past two years. And Shawna had been living in Los Angeles for at least that long. Was it possible that they didn't know about all this stuff? Perhaps this interest in smut had only surfaced once he had passed into puberty.

Jeff put everything back just the way it was and left the room making sure to latch the door tightly behind him. Now he had more things to ask Shawna about—more questions about her family. He had never experienced anything like this. If he told her what he had found, she would know that he was snooping. Then she might wonder what kind of person he himself was to go rifling through a complete stranger's room when he had just been told under no uncertain terms to "stay out". He desperately needed to vent all of his newly discovered knowledge to Kevin as soon as he got home. And that could not be soon enough for him.

He finished the living room and the bathroom and Shawna was done with hers, so all that was left was Ellen's room…and Jared's room. Jeff had noticed a few packed boxes, but other than that, it did not look as though Jared had done much to get his room packed up. What was he doing all the previous day? And where had he gone during the night? He and Shawna had gotten up at 5:30 and he was out already… or still.

When they returned from their visit with their mother, Jeff had already made a good dent on Ellen's room. "Wow! You've gotten almost everything done. How can I thank you enough, Jeff?" Shawna raved.

"Oh, I'll think of something," he answered not even looking up from his task of placing clothing in boxes.

She giggled. "Well, let me help you. I'll put mom's important papers from her file cabinet into these boxes. I already called the real estate man. He's coming today. I told him that we have to leave tomorrow evening to go back to work."

"Can he list it that quickly?"

"He's been out here before... the last time I came home. He said there would be no problem—my not being here. He'll call with any questions or offers."

"Is Jared almost packed?" he asked her, trying to hide his guilty face.

"I told him anything that's not in a labeled box is going into the trash tonight. I can hear him throwing things around in there. He must be frantic to get done by this evening. He knows I'm serious. I said, 'if you like your stuff and want to keep it, better get busy.'"

If you only knew how much he likes his "stuff" and how much he wants to keep it, Jeff thought. He could just picture Jared's boxes being labeled "smut magazines" and "snuff films." But he continued to work as did Shawna and they finished Ellen's room in less than an hour. Everything was done.

They were sitting in the kitchen drinking iced tea when Mark Neiderhelm, the real estate agent, knocked on the door. Shawna introduced the two and he walked in and out of the rooms. "I think I'll be able to sell it furnished like you requested. I have several first-time buyers that don't have any furniture. I'll start bringing them by tomorrow. It looks like this is just what they want. Of course, I haven't seen your brother's room yet, but I know how teenagers are. Got one of my own. As long as my clients can go in there by tomorrow."

"It'll be empty and ready," Shawna reassured him. "And whatever furniture the buyers don't want, just toss it or give it to the mission.

"Good enough."

He sat down at the kitchen table where they filled out some papers. Then he shook hands with Jeff and said, "Hey, you've got a good looking fellow here. You sure make a striking couple, the two of you. I wish you the best." They both blushed as they said "Good-bye."

"You must have so many memories here, huh?"

She nodded. "All kinds of memories. Some wonderful—carefree. Some dreadful." Her eyes glazed over and it looked to Jeff like she was trying hard not to recall some things.

"That bad? Tell me about it."

"I guess all children have a few ghastly memories."

"Did they have to do with your parents?"

"No. My parents were the sweetest people in the world. I don't remember ever hearing a harsh word from either of them. I love them so much. I just can't believe that I'm losing my dear mother. It's just starting to hit me that I won't be able to call her on the phone anymore. No more of our long conversations. There's gonna be a huge hole in my life without her. I still haven't gotten over losing my dad… and now my mom."

"How did your dad die?"

"An accident. I'll tell you about it some time—not right now. I'm too emotional right now." Tears glistened in her eyes and she felt too weak to try to hold them back. Jeff held her hand as she broke into sobs.

The next afternoon, Jeff and Shawna stopped one last time to visit Ellen on their way to the airport. Jared had his mother's car packed up to make the trip to his sister's place in California. That way he would have a car when he got there. Ellen had given the car to Jared when she became too sick to drive anymore. They figured he would arrive sometime Wednesday. All of the boxes were being shipped.

CHAPTER 14

When Jeff walked through his front door, little paws all over his legs and dozens of doggy kisses greeted him. "Oh Duffy, I missed my doggy so much." He picked up the squirming little ball and hugged and kissed him like he'd been gone for a year.

"How'd it go?" Kevin, who always stayed at Jeff's house to puppy-sit when Jeff went on trips, was standing in the doorway to the den with a mug of beer in his hand.

"You are a sight for sore eyes. We have to sit down and talk."

"Somehow, I knew you'd come home with juicy stuff to tell."

Jeff poured each of them a glass of wine and they sat down at the dining room table.

"First of all, her mother looks bad. She's not gonna live much longer."

"Oh, that's hard. How's Shawna taking it?"

"It's tearing her up. But that's not what I have to tell you." Kevin's eyes widened. "It's her brother, Jared. Kev, when I first saw him, I almost jumped three feet in the air."

"Why, was he wearing a pink mini dress and five-inch stilettos?"

Jeff shook his head. "Remember that movie, *Night of the Living Dead?*"

"Of course."

"He looked like he got a hold of one of those zombie masks

and put it on. I kid you not. And he's weird, Kev. I couldn't engage him in any kind of conversation to save my life. He's a complete social cripple."

"Well, Shawna was kinda' like that at the beginning, remember?"

"Oh, she was nothing like this kid. She was shy and inexperienced. Now we never run out of things to talk about. She's so easy to be with—but Jared. I think he wrote the book, *How to Lose Friends and Alienate People*."

"A little off putting, huh?"

Jeff let out a gut laugh. "Off putting? Just think about the scariest "B" horror movie you've ever seen."

"Hmmm, that bad?"

"No, worse."

"Well, maybe he's just a typical teenager. You know what an attitude they can cop."

"Oh no," Jeff said, now frantically shaking his head. "There's more. I snuck into his bedroom while they went to visit their mother…"

"You snooped? Again?"

"I couldn't help it. And I'm glad I did. His room was filled with hard-core porn. I mean really hard-core." He told Kevin everything that he had found.

"No shit! Does Shawna know?"

"About the porn? I don't think so. I don't think anyone's ever been in that room. I can tell you, no one's cleaned it since the house was built."

"Are you gonna tell Shawna what you found?"

"I can't. Then she'll know I was snooping."

"Haven't we had this exact conversation before?"

"Maybe—I don't know. But what should I do?"

"Do you think he's dangerous?"

"It would make you wonder, wouldn't it?"

"Maybe you should tell the police or someone."

"They won't do anything unless he commits some crime. If I tell 'em to come cause he looks weird and he's hiding porno in his room, they'll laugh in my face."

"Jeffrey, my buddy, I'm not gonna beat around the dance floor. Didn't I tell you this chick was trouble? I smelled a rat right from the start. Now we know she comes from the *Addam's Family*." Kevin exclaimed as he made quote signs with his fingers.

"Do you still think I'm crazy for sticking it out with her?"

"Sure, I do."

They talked into the night and Kevin slept over again in one of the guest rooms.

For the next three days, Jeff was, once again, determined to cool things off with Shawna. As much as he was head over heels, he had to agree with Kevin—the situation just kept getting more bizarre by the minute.

One thing that did divert his thoughts from Shawna was that his remote-control action figure project was turning into a smashing success. From the moment the company put the toy into stores, they couldn't keep it on the shelves. They couldn't turn them out fast enough and they thanked Jeff with a big, fat bonus and heaps of praise. It was just the ego stroke that he needed right now.

That Friday, Jeff was starting a new project—a devise that returned a basketball automatically to the player so that he would be better able to practice his free throws.

If he made the shot, the ball would fling right back to him so that he did not have to run all over retrieving it. He had already thought of a name for this gimmicky device—the "Basketball Boomerang."

"Jeff, a call for you on line one. It's Shawna," Ginny informed.

He knew she would call eventually. She always did. "Hi, what's happening?" he asked. He had to admit he felt his heart pounding in his chest as soon as he heard her voice.

"My mother passed away last night."

"Oh no!" He was overwrought with shame. He should have called her immediately after they got home last Monday. "Oh honey, what can I do?"

"I'm having her body cremated and the ashes sent down here. We'll have a service on Sunday—I've chartered a boat. She always said she wanted her ashes scattered at sea." She was speaking through tears, Jeff could tell. How could he have ignored her in her time of need? What a selfish bastard he was. He would never do this to her again. He made a vow to himself right there on the spot that he would give his all to this relationship. He loved her so much. And she hadn't done anything wrong. You don't dump a wonderful woman just because she has an eccentric brother. All right, a fucking lunatic brother.

"Do you want me to come over tonight? To be with you?"

"Oh, I'm trying to get Jared settled into the den. I guess that'll be his room from now on. I've got to get my stuff out to make room for him. You know, his computer and whatever junk he keeps."

Oh boy, do I know the junk he keeps, Jeff thought. But instead, he asked, "Can I help with anything?"

"That's so sweet of you. There is something. Would you be able to store some of these boxes in your garage? I put as many as I could fit into my storage bin, but there are about ten more that I don't have room for. If it's a problem, I can rent a storage space."

"I have plenty of room in my garage. I'll bring a van from work. Should I come tonight?"

"That'd be great. I'll have dinner ready for you. I've taken two weeks off to get all of this squared away."

"I'll be there about seven?"

"Thank you."

"I love you, sweetheart."

"I love you, Jeff… so much."

He knew that he was making a major commitment by storing her stuff at his house, but what could he say... after the way he had ignored her since their trip up North.

Shawna cooked Cornish game hens stuffed with wild rice and mushrooms. Jared grabbed his plate from the table and took it into his room to eat. Even though it was rude behavior, Jeff was secretly glad to have his dinner alone with Shawna. Glad not to have to see or smell that kid.

"He's just rude that way, Jeff. Don't take it personally. He's equally rude to everyone... even me."

"It doesn't bother me. I'm glad to be alone with you."

"Me too," she whispered.

"Do you want to come and stay with me tonight?" he asked. "After we bring the boxes over?"

"There's nothing I would love more, but I'm a little worried about leaving Jared here by himself."

"He's seventeen, for Christ's sake. You don't have to baby-sit him anymore, do you?" He recoiled at his own bad-mannered response. "I didn't mean that the way it came out, honey. It's just that I thought once I reached thirty, child care would be behind me."

"No, you're right. I'm being ridiculous. We're gonna live our lives the same as we did before he came to live with me. I have to get over this feeling that he needs to be watched all the time. My parents were that way with him and I guess it rubbed off on me."

Jeff was again consumed with guilt feelings for he knew that Jared did, indeed, need to be watched... all the time! What if he were to hurt someone? Who really knew what he was capable of? Then it would be partially his fault. No, it would be all his fault. He knew things about Jared that even Shawna didn't know.

"I don't know what's the matter with me. Here I go just thinking of myself. Do you want to invite him to spend the night at my house? In one of the guest rooms?"

"He won't come," she said. "He's already making an asylum out of my den—just like his room at home."

Thank God! he thought, immediately regretting his offer. He was even afraid for Duffy's safety if Jared were to be under his roof. His thoughts began to go wild and he had fantasies of killing Jared if he were to harm one little hair on Duffy's body.

"I understand. You take your time. I won't pressure you in any way. That's the last thing you need. We'll talk about this later on… after your mother's service. Okay?"

"Okay."

CHAPTER 15

The service was quite lovely just off the coast in a chartered boat with a minister speaking poignant words of love, life and eternal happiness. Shawna got up and spoke about being blessed with such a warm and compassionate mother. She told of how Ellen thought of everyone before herself. How very close they had always been. How now, Ellen would be with Phillip, her beloved husband for all eternity. Then, they scattered her ashes and at the same moment, each person threw orchids (Ellen's favorite flower) into the ocean. Jeff held Shawna as she sobbed. Jared showed no emotion whatsoever. No tears. No words. He just sat with his eyes looking out at the rippling ocean seeming to be a million miles away, immersed in that distant world of his. *That sick, perverted world,* Jeff thought.

When they returned to Shawna's apartment, she told Jeff, "I need to stay close to you tonight. Is it okay if I follow you to your house, then I can just come home later in the day tomorrow?"

"Of course it's okay. I'm so glad you're ready to stay with me."

"I'm not my brother's keeper. I can't spend my life being a slave to him like mom did. He has to take responsibility for himself. That's the only way he'll ever grow up. He has his computer to keep him company. He spends most of his time online anyway. I'm going home with my love."

Jeff smiled with admiration in his eyes.

They had what could only be described as a spiritual experience that night. A night Jeff would never forget. They shared feelings. They communicated ideas about life after death. They bared their souls to each other. They made love…love like nothing Jeff had ever known. Shawna had opened herself to him in the deepest and most unguarded manner.

"I have no doubt that you are my soul mate," he whispered in her ear as they lay in each other's arms. "I never thought it was possible to feel this close to another human being."

"Neither did I. You are my first and only love."

He felt a surge pulsating through his body with the warm awareness that he had been her only love.

He kissed her goodbye when he left for work early the next morning. Shawna slept until 12:30 PM. She had desperately needed this indulgence. She hadn't had good night's sleep in weeks.

When she arrived home, Jared was in his room so she banged on the door. "Jared, can I come in? I have to talk with you."

She could hear some frantic scrambling in there, then after about a minute, he opened the door and came out, closing it behind him. His face was marked with what appeared to be scratches down his left cheek.

"What happened to your face?"

"Oh, my skin was itching. I guess I scratched too hard in my sleep or something."

"Yeah, I guess you did. Anyway, Jared, things are gonna change from now on. If you're not going to school, you're gonna have to get a job. You're not sitting around on your butt like you did with Mom. I want you to get settled in a job and eventually look for your own place. You can't stay here forever. What's to become of you? You have got to start planning a future for yourself."

"What kind a' job?"

"Anything. You know computers really well. Why don't you explore that field, even if you have to take some classes. I swear, little brother, I've never seen anyone, much less a man, have less gumption and enthusiasm for life than you!"

"What do I do… to get a job?"

"Well, you could start with the Internet. They have job sites, don't they?"

"Yeah."

"Well, get busy. And I'm going to clean you up and get you some decent clothes. No one's gonna hire you looking and smelling like that."

"Whatever."

"And one thing for sure, you're going to a dentist. I'm making you an appointment right now." This last bit of information was met with stunned silence. Jared had only been to a dentist once in his life and that was when he was nine years old. But, the experience was permanently etched in his memory cells. An agonizing event where they stuck needles into his gums, drilled, dug and scraped and any other torture they could think up. From that day on, every time Ellen would mention a trip to the dentist, he would yell and scream and stomp his feet in a blatant refusal to go. If this method failed, he would simply disappear on the day of his scheduled visit. But, his big sister was not going to be so easily manipulated… he could see that right away.

Much to his relief, the first appointment Shawna's dentist had open was two months away. That would give him time to plan his "getaway" strategy.

"I'm not like Mom," she started right in again. " I won't allow you to hide away in your room for the rest of your life. I'm pushing you out of the nest and you'll thank me for it someday. And you're gonna start learning some social skills. You've got to learn to get along with people."

"I don't like people—they don't like me. Never did—never will."

"That's because you've alienated people all your life, but it's going to stop right now. Go take a shower. I'm taking you to get a haircut and then we're going shopping for a new wardrobe. Get going!"

"Shawn, you're already a nag. I knew you would be. Mom never got on my case."

"God damn it, Jared, Mom stopped trying to help you! Mom and Dad did everything under the sun to help you fit in with your peers. You rebelled against everything that was done for you. They finally gave up."

"I was fine living with Mom. Why can't you just leave me alone?"

"You're not getting away with that shit in my home. You're lucky to be here, brother. And if you don't abide by my rules, there are a lot of halfway houses and shelters you can go to. If you don't fit in there, there're always the streets. It's shape up or ship out."

Jared took a shower and put his ratty clothes back on. It seemed as if he had no interest in hygiene whatsoever. Shawna took him out for a major overhaul. She supervised his haircut and it looked pretty decent when the barber finished. She had instructed him to cut it short... wash and wear. "WASH and wear," she reiterated to Jared. She bought him a lot of nice pants and shirts—underwear and shoes. She also bought him some skin care products in order to get that hideous acne under control. She had never once known him to even wash his face. When she was done, he actually resembled a human being... in a creepy sort of way. When they got home that night, she forced him to eat dinner with her at the table where she harassed him so much about his manners; he almost lost his temper with her—something he had never done.

She was on a quest to keep him from closing himself up in his room. They watched TV together in the living room; however, she could plainly see that he was very uneasy, chomping at the bit to escape to the refuge of his "sanctuary"... especially after the ordeal he had been put through all day.

On the evening news, one of the top stories was about a murdered fourteen-year-old. "High school student raped and brutally slain," the reporter read. "Her half-clad body was found dumped in the foothills of Glendale."

"What kind of a sick bastard would do that to a young innocent girl?" She addressed her question to the universe. Jared said nothing.

"Can I go to my room now?" he finally asked.

"You're impossible. Okay, but I want you to call some of the ads I have circled in the paper for a job first thing in the morning. Maybe you can set up some interviews for this week."

"Aw, fuck!"

"I'm knocking on your door at nine o'clock sharp—no sleeping the day away around here." She almost felt a little guilty making this demand on him since sleeping late was one of her favorite indulgences. But then, she told herself, I work for a living, damn it! I deserve to treat myself once in a while. He sleeps on and off all day long.

He stomped into his room and slammed the door shut.

CHAPTER 16

To Jared's dismay, his big sister stood over him like a drill sergeant while he dialed up the third number on her long list of job possibilities. She started right in with her badgering, "Honey, your voice sounds way too lifeless... you know, too deadpan. It almost sounds like you're saying 'You don't want to hire me, do you?' You need to speak with more inflection... more lilt," she instructed with an upward sweep of her palm. Each time he picked up the phone he felt like there was a mad conductor standing in front of him—mouthing directives, hands flapping in the air. He punched out the next number on her exhaustive list and went directly back to his apathetic monotone. Shawna gave an exasperated shrug and surrendered to defeat.

After about twenty-five phone calls Jared did set up one job interview. It was for a laborer at a paper mill on the outskirts of the city. He would be performing various tasks such as: operating a forklift to stock and pull down huge rolls of paper, general maintenance around the plant, filling and emptying vats of chemicals and whatever else they needed him to do.

Shawna inspected him before he left for his interview. "Well, you could look better, but you could look a lot worse. Go ahead. And Jared, don't just sit there like a bump on a log. Show some enthusiasm. Talk about your interests and put some expression into it—be animated. Ask the man questions about the company. You know, if there's any chance for advancement, what the salary is. Stuff like that, okay?"

"Uh huh."

He came home three hours later and told her he got the job. "They hired you?" she almost screamed it. "When do you start?"

"Monday, but I don't know."

"You don't know what?"

"I don't think I'm gonna like it."

"Oh yes you are. It's a job and you're gonna like it. Jared, don't you even care about earning a paycheck? I can't keep giving you money like mom did. You've got to make your own way in this world. Do you understand what I'm telling you?"

"Huh?"

"Are you listening?" she barked. "After all, I might get married some day—then where would you go?"

"Couldn't I go with you?"

"NO!"

Shawna had a date with Jeff the next Saturday for another round of antiquing. She was excited for they always had so much fun sharing this activity.

She drove to his house so that she could spend the night. She brought an overnight case and a nice dress to change into for dinner that evening. Jeff had made reservations at a ritzy restaurant in Beverly Hills. She couldn't wait. She had never been to a place this fancy.

The day was sunny, but cool so they both dressed in sweaters and long pants. As they browsed and shopped at various antique stores in the valley, she apprised Jeff of everything she had been through with Jared during the previous week.

"You really got him to clean up?"

"Yeah, but I had to stay on him 'cause the minute I left him unattended, he slipped back into his old clothes."

"It looks like you're making genuine progress. I'm proud of you, standing up to him and taking the bull by the horns. He needs that. This job might give him the self-confidence he's lacking."

"I sure hope he doesn't blow it, Jeff. He has a way of sabotaging any situation he doesn't like. If this doesn't work, I don't know what I'm gonna do with him. I really don't want him living in my house forever."

"Neither do I," Jeff admitted.

Her eyes danced as she flashed him a grin. "I thought he would put you off a bit. Were you surprised that I have a brother like him?"

"Surprised? I thought it was some kind of a joke at first—like the two of you were pulling a prank on me. He's nothing like you. And nothing like your mother. You're both so pretty and sweet. I don't mean to disparage him, really. It's just that it was a major shock when I looked up and saw him standing over me like Dracula that day in your kitchen."

"I know. He's definitely the black sheep of the family… to put it mildly. Dad was finally coming down pretty hard on him those few months before his accident, but mom always let him get away with anything. She never seemed to take a firm stand with him… just let him come and go as he pleased. No wonder he was happy living up there with her. He did whatever he wanted—whenever he wanted."

"How did your father pass away, Shawna? I'm not pressuring you—you don't have to answer if it makes you uncomfortable. I'm just curious."

"No, I think I can talk about it now." She cleared her throat and paused for a moment, then spoke in a low, despondent voice, "The roof was leaking that winter and it was dripping into the living room and my bedroom through the ceiling. We had to push the furniture out of the way and put pans down to catch the water. And it kept getting worse—trickling in faster and faster. In no time at all, the pans were changed to buckets and they were filling up in a matter of hours. Well, the rain just kept coming down in sheets. All the roofing companies were up to their eyeballs in repairs so dad got the extension ladder out of the garage and climbed up there to try and patch where it was pouring in."

Her sobs burst out suddenly and it startled Jeff. She had seemed like she was in perfect control when she started telling the story—now, all of a sudden, Niagara Falls.

"I didn't mean to upset you like this," he said as he guided her to sit down at one of the tables just outside a Starbucks coffee shop. "You don't have to tell me this now. I didn't know it was still so fresh—I mean the pain of it."

"I've never talked about it until now."

"Get out! Why the hell not?"

"I don't know. Mom's way of coping with unpleasantries was to avoid them. Never talk about it and it's like it didn't happen."

"Well, take it from a guy who's had lots of therapy, it only festers—eats away at you like a cancer, if you don't work through it."

Her expression changed to one of sudden pensiveness. "And Mom just died of cancer."

Jeff said nothing and there was a long gap of silence that hung between them, then she went on, "I could hear him pounding away up there for about a half an hour, then nothing. The storm was making so much noise that it must have covered up his screams. It was an hour later that Mom started to feel like something was amiss. We thought the pounding had stopped because he came down to get more materials or something. But, it wasn't thirty seconds before I heard Mom's earsplitting shrieks. When I raced out the back door, there was Dad lying faced down on the cement. Mom just kept shrieking and crying so I turned him over and started CPR. But, as soon as I touched his body, I knew for sure he was dead. I kept on though—chest compressions and mouth to mouth. Mom was no help. She was completely hysterical. I finally had to yell at her to call 911. When she loses it, she's gone.

"They pronounced him dead at the scene. Accidental death, it was written on his death certificate. Slipped on the wet tiles and took a fatal fall. I left for California three weeks after the funeral."

Jeff was holding both of her hands tightly. "How awful for you. Having to see him like that. You really loved him didn't you?"

"I was Daddy's little girl. I loved him so much. I've never been able to stop the nagging voice in my head—if only I'd gone to check on him sooner. Was he alive for part of that hour? Had he lain there dying for forty-five minutes?"

"It wasn't your fault at all, honey. How in the world could you have known he was in trouble? And, I'm sure he died on impact—probably never knew what hit him. I don't think he suffered for one minute." He had no idea if any of this were true, but why torture herself about it for the rest of her life when it was over now? What earthly good could it do to blame herself? "Are you glad you told me?"

She nodded and when she did, she looked just like a small child sitting there. He kissed both of her hands and went in to buy each of them a frosted mocha. They sat for a while talking about her ordeal and that there was nothing anyone could have done that would have changed the outcome.

Jeff had it timed perfectly. They would need to be back at his house at five o'clock to get ready for dinner at seven. He changed into a gorgeous deep gray suit with rose-colored pin strips. Underneath, he wore a pale pink shirt with a gray and ruby colored tie. Shawna put on a pure silk, rose and black cocktail dress that displayed her voluptuous cleavage and her lovely back.

She threw a warm shawl over her shoulders as the weather was becoming quite chilly at night.

"You look so handsome," she told him.

"And you're so beautiful," he returned. "You do a lot for that dress."

The restaurant was elegant to say the least. There was a girl to check their coats as soon as they stepped in the door. The Matre'd greeted them, "Good evening Mr. Daniels, Miss Reese. May I show you to your table?"

He sat them in a cozy, private booth. The lighting was soft and the table was set with exquisite crystal wine glasses and glistening silverware. There was a candle burning in a cherry-colored glass and a single rose showed off its lavender blush from a small, porcelain vase. A man dressed in a white tux was playing beautiful melodies on a grand piano across the room. It was a fairy tale date for Shawna.

"I feel like a princess with my knight in shining armor."

"Am I your knight in shining armor?"

"Yes," she said as she leaned in to softly kiss his lips.

Jeff ordered a fabulous Pinot Noir and then they decided on their dinners. Shawna ordered pheasant and Jeff ordered Chilean sea bass. The cuisine and the service were extraordinary. They talked, they kissed, they gazed deeply into each other's eyes.

"This is the most romantic night of my life," she told Jeff.

"It is for me as well," he smiled tenderly. "I'm so thankful that you slopped your drink all over me that first night. We may not be sitting here right now if you hadn't."

Her whole body was overcome with a wave of goose bumps. "I can't imagine my life without you."

Jeff saw her eyes mist and he knew she was heartfelt in her emotions. How could this have happened to him so quickly after losing Amber? But these feelings were brand new to him. He knew now, that he had never really been in love before. What he was feeling for Shawna was the "Real McCoy."

Shawna spent an amazing night with Jeff and she stayed most of the day on Sunday. They, again, slept in, read the paper and Jeff served breakfast in bed. In the afternoon, they took Duffy for a long walk. It could not have been more perfect—more romantic.

She arrived back at her apartment in the evening to find that Jared was out. She thought this would be a perfect opportunity to go through his closet and bag up his old clothes to throw into the dumpster. That way, he wouldn't be able to revert to his old dress habits.

She snapped the light on in his room and looked around. "He's gonna be furious when he finds out I came into his room. But, hell, it's my house!"

She laid some large trash bags next to his closet and went to work pulling out old, foul-smelling clothing that she was sure had not been washed in months. "Teenagers!" she said aloud.

But as she emptied a good part of the closet, something caught her eye. "I must be seeing things." She bent down and grabbed a pile of magazines that had been stacked way back into a corner of the closet under a pile of dirty clothes. "Jesus Christ!" she screamed. She began leafing through the pages in utter disbelief. "This is vile… revolting. Way beyond pornography. Only a sick mind would look at this filth."

"Oh my God, Mom, Jared is a pervert!" she cried looking up to the heavens. Through her rage, she finished stuffing all of his old clothing into the bags. Then she gathered all of the magazines and threw them on the coffee table in the living room. She sat down on the sofa to wait for him to come home.

CHAPTER 17

It was 10 PM when the door opened and Jared walked in. He jumped when he saw her sitting there—arms crossed, trembling—with daggers in her eyes. "Where the hell have you been?"

"Just out. I went to the mall to get some things."

"What things? Where are the bags?"

"I couldn't find what I wanted."

"Oh? Then did you go peeping in girls windows again?"

"Who told you…?" Just then he lowered his gaze and saw his reading material stacked on the coffee table. "You were in my room!" he shouted. "God dammit, I told you to stay outta' my room!"

"I went in there to sort through your clothes—to throw out all of that old crap and I found this smut on your closet floor. What are you doing with this?!" she screamed as she picked up one of the magazines and waved it in his face. He was silent.

"You're sick! You're insane! What the hell's the matter with you?"

"That's just old junk some guy in school gave me a long time ago. I guess I forgot to throw it out. I only looked at it out of curiosity, then I forgot all about it." He actually looked nervous.

"How long ago did this 'guy' give these to you?"

"I don't know. Back when I was in school."

"Well, that's interesting because some of them are dated only two months ago. What the hell are you into, Jared?"

"Nothing. I was just curious, okay? I'll get rid of 'em."

"I'll say you will—right this instant!" She got up and stuffed all of the magazines into one of the large trash bags. "Is this all or are there more someplace?"

"That's all," he said with his eyes fixed on the floor.

She walked over to him and squeezed his cheeks as hard as she could. "You will never bring disgusting shit like this into my home again. Understand?"

"Yeah."

She carried the bag downstairs and threw it into the dumpster. He was lying about where he was all evening and he was lying about the magazines. What, in God's name, was going on in that twisted mind of his?

"Did Mom know about this stuff?" she asked when she walked back into the apartment.

"No. She never came in my room."

"Never? Not even to clean?"

"No. I told her it was my private domain and she respected that."

"And by respecting your request, she allowed something like this to be under her roof. I would say that's bad parenting. She must be turning over in her grave, Jared."

"Are you done yellin' at me?"

"Yes. Jared, you're my baby brother and I love you, but at this minute I'm completely ashamed of you."

"I'm goin' to bed. Night, Shawna." He went into his room and shut the door.

Shawna was so distraught there was no way she would be able to fall asleep for a while… if at all. She climbed into bed and clicked on the TV to watch the eleven o'clock news. The top story was another murder. This time a body was found dumped over the side of Mulholland Drive. They said the body was fresh—probably killed Saturday night sometime. It bore similarities to the murder in Glendale the previous week.

They went on to say that the body found a week ago had been bludgeoned to death with a large blunt object. The girl had been sexually assaulted prior to her death. They said that more information would be forthcoming as it became available.

Shawna cringed. "Oh, I'm off the deep end even thinking what I'm thinking." She told herself she was just upset over the magazines. Jared was just a kid. She tossed and turned all night, not getting even ten minutes of sleep.

Jeff called her at her work the next day to tell her what a perfectly glorious weekend he had had with her and it was just what she needed to hear after all of the ugliness of Sunday night. She thought about telling him what she had found in Jared's room, but did not want to break the loving spell between them. They reminisced their romantic weekend and made a date for mid-week. Jeff had long time plans with Kevin to play in an out-of-town golf tournament the next weekend. "I can't go two weeks without seeing you, so how about dinner Wednesday night after we get off work?"

"How about Pedro's? I've always wanted to try it. You and Kevin rave about it so much."

"Ummm…I'm always up for Pedro's. Pick you up at six?"

"I can't wait."

CHAPTER 18

For the next two days, Shawna was shaking so much from nerves; she had a hard time focusing on her work. Should she confide her discovery to Jeff or should she keep it a secret? No, she thought. My nerves can't survive any more secrets. I'm in love with Jeff and he needs to know what I'm going through in my life. Isn't that what love is all about? Being there for each other in the dark times as well as the light? She decided that their feelings were now strong enough to weather some harsh reality.

Pedro's was bustling with business. The hostess seated them in a booth. "Is this place always this busy?" she asked scanning the room.

"Every night. You should see it on the weekends. You can't even move in here. Kev and I always have to wait at least an hour on Friday and Saturday."

"I think I'll run to the restroom, honey… before we order."

"Through the bar to your right," he instructed.

When she came out, some other people were sitting at their table. She panicked for a second, then spotted Jeff at a table across the restaurant frantically waving her down. She looked to see that a family with a baby in a high chair had been seated right next to their original table. This was something that happened on a regular basis with Jeff. When she came out of a restroom, she often had to track Jeff to another part of the restaurant when small children had taken up residence in close proximity. He would gather up all of their dishes, drinks and silverware and just move to get away from potential pandemonium. On occasion, it happened more than once in the same evening.

She smiled and waved back at him making her way to the farthest table he could find away from baby.

Shawna ordered enchiladas rancheras and Jeff ordered a combo of a chicken taco and cheese tamale. They sat devouring their tasty food for a while, then Shawna leaned in for a serious discussion.

"I'm having problems with Jared. I went into his room to throw out his old clothes and you'll die when you hear what I stumbled across."

"What... what did you find?"

"Pornographic magazines that were so bad, I can't even tell you what was in them."

"Then you didn't see the videos?" The words flew out of his mouth so fast, he didn't even know it was he who had spoken them. They both sat staring at each other—eyes wide and jaws dropped.

When a solid thought finally took form in Shawna's head, she asked, "What do you mean, videos?"

"Oh honey, I have a confession to make. That day, when you and Jared went to visit your mother, I snooped in his room. I'm sorry, I'm sorry, I'm sorry!"

"Why Jeffrey Daniels," she snickered. "You actually have a lot more guts than Mom ever had. She never set foot in that room. Then you saw the magazines?"

"Oh yeah!"

"Why didn't you tell me?"

"And admit that I'm a lowdown, sneaking buttinsky? I don't think so."

"When were you gonna tell me I have a sexual deviant for a brother? And what about videos tapes?"

He reached across the table and took both of her hands in

his. "Honey, I found porno videos too. Not just porno, though. Horrible stuff. Unspeakable stuff."

"How horrible?"

"I think as bad as it could get. Have you ever heard of snuff films?"

Shawna gasped as her hands flew to her mouth. "Oh no, Jeff. You must be mistaken. Jared might be touched in the head, but that's too much. I can't believe he would look at anything so evil as that."

"Maybe I'm mistaken. I was only in there for a few minutes. I must have read it wrong."

"What do you think we should do? Search his room more thoroughly when he's out?"

Ah, she was coming around to his way of thinking. "Well, that wouldn't be a bad idea. That way, at least we'll know one way or the other what he's got in there," he suggested. "And Shawna, please don't tell him where I live."

She flashed him an understanding smile. "I certainly won't. I'll go through the apartment to make sure there's nothing with your address or phone number on it. I'll do that right away tonight," she reassured him. "Jeff, you've been so wonderful and supportive through all of this. I don't know of any other man who would stick around with a girl who had a brother like mine."

"It seems like both of us are always apologizing for our families, doesn't it?"

"It does," she agreed. "Putting up with crazy relatives. Only yours are cute and funny—mine is vile and disgusting."

He gave her a concerned smile.

Shawna stayed home the next weekend and kept a low profile. She never mentioned the magazines again and certainly did not bring up Jeff's discovery of any videotapes. She kept herself busy around the house and cooked some nice meals for

Jared and her. Again, she had to work hard to get him to stay in the main part of the house with her. On the rare occasions when he did come out, his impatience to return to his room was palpable.

She did manage to ask him about his new job. "How did you like it?"

"Not much."

"What did they have you do?"

"Everything. Hard stuff they don't wanna do."

"Were the people nice?"

"I don't know. They just told me what to do and I did it."

"You're gonna stay, aren't you?"

"I guess."

"Jared, you need to think about going back to school or at least learning a trade. If you don't, you're gonna be stuck in jobs like this for the rest of your life."

"Ah huh."

Spending the entire weekend at home, cooped up with Jared was certainly not what Shawna would have preferred. She wanted to go shopping for some new winter clothes, but she was not about to leave Jared alone, even for ten minutes.

Jared did not leave the apartment at all until he left for work Monday morning. He knew that his sister would have given him the third degree about where he was going and what he was doing. She was quickly becoming a major thorn in his side.

CHAPTER 19

Jeff and Kevin checked in to their hotel near the golf course where they would play in a two-day tournament in San Diego. A burst of stale air hit their nostrils as soon as they stepped into their room. The two queen-sized beds that sat side by side were covered with thin quilts that looked old. There were stains on the carpet and the wallpaper was pulling away from the corners near the ceiling

"Oh shit, let's open the slider," Jeff bristled. "Get some fresh air in here. How much did we pay for this place?"

"Three-fifty a night."

"Why the hell so much?"

"They said it's a four-star hotel," Kevin informed.

Jeff looked around the room, "Four stars out of how many... nineteen?"

"Oh, what the hell," Kevin said. "We're here now and it's the closest one I could find to the golf course that had anything available for this weekend."

"That's what we get for waiting till the last minute to make reservations. Next time, I make the accommodation arrangements."

"Fine with me, Mister Persnickety," Kevin jabbed.

"Let's unpack and go down and get some dinner," Jeff suggested.

"Sounds good to me, I'm starved."

They both emptied out their bags, Kevin stuffing everything into drawers—Jeff carefully hanging up his neatly pressed golf shirts and slacks in the closet.

"You iron all that stuff yourself?" Kevin inquired.

"No, I send it out to be dry cleaned."

"Your shirts, pants, everything?"

"Yes. It's the only way to keep them looking nice," Jeff lectured. "Once you wash something, it never looks decent again. Don't you ever get your clothes dry cleaned?"

"Not unless it has a tag that says "DRY CLEAN ONLY." If it has washing instructions, I wash it."

Kevin watched his buddy with disbelief as he precisely placed, even his impeccably folded underwear into the bottom drawer of the cabinet that also held the television set.

"You are some goddamned piece o' work, Jeffrey."

Jeff slid open the two top drawers where Kevin had crammed all of his clothing. "YOU are the piece of work. Look how you keep your things—all shoved together in a wad. How do you even find anything in this mess?"

"Oh, I know where my stuff is. I'm just glad I'm not all finicky like you. I wouldn't be able to stand myself."

"You're gonna look all wrinkled and unkempt on the golf course tomorrow," Jeff ribbed.

"And you're gonna look like you stepped out of Gentleman's Quarterly. And that's gonna take strokes off your game... how?"

Jeff couldn't hold back his gut laugh.

As they ate their dinner (which was marginal according to Jeff), he apprised Kevin of all the Jared news up to date.

"You blurted out about the videos?"

"Can you believe it? It flew out of my mouth without even stopping to think. I was forced to level with her about poking my nose in where it doesn't belong. But Kev, that's how you find things out. Since she found the magazines and I told her about the tapes, she's becoming really suspicious about Jared. She's starting to see just how sick he actually is."

"What are you gonna do about it?"

"We're gonna search his room with a fine-tooth comb while he's at work. We're both gonna take a day off to do it. That way we can take our time and not have to be afraid of getting caught."

"Jesus. When are you planning this covert operation?"

"Next Thursday."

"Do you want some help? I'll be the lookout. I could hide down by the carport and watch to make sure he doesn't come home. We could use the walkie talkies on our cell phonies."

Jeff chuckled. "Would you do that?"

"Yeah. I'll call up to you as soon as I see his car coming."

"Okay. We could use a lookout. I'll make sure it's all right with Shawna."

Their foursome finished in second place and Kevin won the longest drive contest. Jeff had left Duffy with his parents for the weekend—his second choice of babysitters.

Thursday morning, when Jared left for work, Shawna walked down with him and got into her car pretending to go to her job as usual. She drove to the designated meeting place—the parking lot of a nearby supermarket. Jeff and Kevin were already waiting.

"Hi honey, you remember Kevin… from the party?"

"Yes. This is nice of you to help us, Kevin. You must think we're crazy, huh?"

"No. Jeff told me about the material you found in his room. I think you're doing the right thing here."

Even though Kevin and Shawna worked for the same company, they never crossed paths at work. This was only the second time she had laid eyes on him. And here he was helping in a clandestine sting against her little brother.

"What kind of car does he drive?" Kevin asked.

"A '98 Honda Accord—silver," Shawna replied.

Kevin stood watch where he could see what cars were coming and still not be exposed. He was glad there was a huge oleander bush he could hide behind while he peeked through the open spaces between the leaves. I hope he doesn't see me, he thought to himself. I hope nobody sees me. I must look like some kinda nutcase hiding in this bush.

Shawna and Jeff dug into the room in question—Jeff starting with the closet, Shawna pulling things out of dresser drawers. After a time, Jeff stuck his head out, "Does Jared play baseball?"

"Are you kidding? He's never played one sport in his whole life."

"Then what are these doing in here?" he asked as he held up four brand new bats.

Her eyes widened, "I don't know. What could he be doing with those?"

"Let's don't jump to any conclusions. Maybe they were a birthday gift or something."

"It's the 'or something' I'm worried about."

"We'll find out. We need to conduct our investigation without raising suspicion. If he thinks we're on to him, he'll hide everything in some other place and then we'll never know what he's up to."

"You're right about that."

As Jeff resumed his investigation of the closet, he noticed several stacks of dark colored blankets on the shelf above the clothing rack. "Honey, what does he need all these blankets for? Does he get that cold?"

She peeked her head in to take a look. "I don't know. Maybe he brought them from home. It gets really cold where we lived, but why would he need so many?"

"It's probably nothing," Jeff said. "Just his stuff from his room at home."

"Oh God!" Shawna cried out when she resumed her search. "Here're those tapes you saw." Her body went cold as she flipped through the videos, dropping them on the floor as if she would be poisoned by the touch of them.

"They were in the exact same cabinet when I was in his room back at your house," Jeff told her. "I can't believe he would be this careless about leaving them in such an easy to find spot. Especially after he knows you were already in his room a few nights ago."

"What do I do with them?"

"Put 'em back exactly the way you found them. He probably knows every one of them backwards and forwards. This search is to gain more insight. We can't let him know we were in here. That would ruin everything."

"I don't know if I can sleep knowing this disgusting filth is under my roof. But now, I don't know if I can sleep knowing Jared's under my roof."

Shawna pulled back the bed covers and shrieked at the top of her voice. There, between the sheets was a noose with the other end of the rope hooked around one of the slats in the headboard, then the frayed end draping back over the pillow... in perfect pulling position.

"Holy shit!" Jeff blurted.

"What is this?" she cried. "Was he trying to kill himself?"

"It's used in auto-erotic practices," Jeff explained. "There are men that hang themselves while they masturbate. They tie the rope around their necks to cut off the oxygen supply to the brain. It's said to heighten the sensation when they reach orgasm. Only thing is, sometimes they accidentally die."

Shawna sat down for a moment to try to digest this information. Her head was spinning with shock and repulsion. Jeff quickly put the bed back together as it was, then booted up Jared's computer and logged on to the Internet. He clicked the mouse on "favorite sites." "Honey, come over here," he said with urgency in his voice. Site after site of hard-core porn popped up.

"He's obsessed with this stuff," she said as tears began to roll down her cheeks. "I had no idea of the extent of his sickness."

Jeff took her into his arms and kissed the top of her head.

"We're gonna get to the bottom of this. Your brother is seriously disturbed, but he has to agree to go the therapy. No one can force him."

"But Mom and Dad sent him to years of therapy. The doctor talked. He stared off into space. It was always a one sided conversation. Do you think he's a psychopath?"

Before Jeff had a chance to answer, Kevin beeped his cell phone. He hastily jammed it to his ear. "What?"

"The subject's driving up! Get the hell out of there. He's pulling into the parking space. Oh shit!"

"Stall him, Kev. Go ask to bum a cigarette or ask directions or something. Give us three minutes."

Kevin walked up just as Jared was opening the door to get out. "Excuse me sir, would you happen to have a smoke?"

"Oh...yeah...I think so." Jared rummaged around in his glove compartment and pulled out a pack of Pall Malls.

"These okay?" he asked the stranger.

"Perfect."

Jared put the pack back in the glove compartment, slid out and closed the door. He started to walk away when the stranger engaged him again. "Do you know if there're any vacancies in this building? I was just walking by and I noticed how nice it looked. I live with my parents a few blocks over that way," he said gesturing to his right.

"No. I don't know. You have to talk to the manager." Again Jared began to walk away.

"You wouldn't know which apartment he lives in, would you?"

"No." Jared was becoming visibly irritated. Kevin tried one more time to ask a question, but Jared ignored him this time, turning his back and walking out of the carport.

Jeff's beeper went off again. "He's coming up the stairs! Are you ready?"

"Shawna, get out of there! He's on the stairs!"

Jared put his key in the lock and opened the door. He jumped when he saw Jeff and Shawna sitting on the couch in the living room. "What are you doing here?" he grunted.

"My car broke down on the way to work this morning," Shawna lied. "I called Jeff to come and help me. We had to wait for the mechanic to change the belts. One of them broke and the others were old. What are you doing home?"

"They let me go. Said I didn't fit in."

"You've got to be kidding. Fit in to a manual labor job like that? I'm calling your boss. This is outrageous."

Jared went to his room and Shawna got on the phone to see if he was telling her the truth. "Mr. Lapinski, this is Jared's sister. He just came home saying he was fired. Is that true?"

"Miss Reese, I did have to let him go. I'm sorry it didn't work out, but he was constantly disappearing. He was always off hiding somewhere when we needed something done. Then, his work performance was extremely slow and sub-standard."

"Thank you," she said and hung up.

"I'd better go," Jeff whispered. "Kev's waiting downstairs. I'll call you later, okay?"

"Okay, sweetheart." She walked him to the door.

Jeff drove his car around to pick up Kevin where he was waiting near the carport. "You weren't blowin' smoke outta your ass. I tried to stall him, but he was so standoffish. Answered in one or two words."

"A bit hard to engage?" Jeff snickered.

Kevin peered over at his buddy and let out a gut laugh. "Hard to engage? The guy made my blood curdle. Now, I see what we're up against."

"You should've seen him before Shawna did an extreme makeover on him."

"I can't even imagine."

Did you have time to get the bedroom back in order?" Kevin asked as he rolled the car window down to throw out the unlit cigarette Jared had given him.

"Barely. We had just sat down on the couch when he came through the door. Thanks so much for your help, Kev. We would've been caught if you hadn't staked out the carport."

"No problem. Anytime you need help. What'd you find?"

"Brand new baseball bats. A hanging noose. I showed Shawna those videos. Then I checked his computer and found all kinds o' porn sites."

"Wait, wait, wait…a hanging noose?!" Kevin shouted. "Is he one of those guys who strangles himself while he jacks off?"

"It appears so," Jeff answered. "How could he be so barefaced, Kevin? Leaving all that stuff around his room."

"He probably doesn't know that his sister is dating the king of the super snoops. He must be pretty confident that his mother and sister would never set foot in his den of iniquity."

"Well, they should have snooped through his belongings years ago. This kid is dangerously troubled."

CHAPTER 20

Shawna watched the news each night for more information on those two murders. It appeared that there were no new victims over the past weekend. The reporter did, however, have new information on the two previous victims. The crimes appeared to have been committed by the same perpetrator. The MO was the same. Both teenage girls—both bludgeoned to death with a large blunt object—both sexually assaulted. The report went on the say that they did collect semen samples that had been sent to the lab for DNA testing.

She tried to push it out of her mind telling herself that she must be jumping to conclusions because of the bombshell that had just dropped on her about Jared's underground lifestyle.

She immediately started in on him to look for another job, but he fought her every inch of the way. And her massive makeover attempt appeared to be coming undone. Now, even his new clothes were becoming ratty and his hair was already hanging in his face in greasy strings. His skin was no better at all, suggesting that he was not using all of the expensive products she had bought for him. She realized that any attempt to make him look presentable was doomed to fail.

Jeff invited her to stay at his place for the weekend and she couldn't have been more eager. Eager to get out of her apartment—away from Jared.

They discussed what to do about Jared, but all conversations on the subject ran into a brick wall. He refused to clean up and try to improve his people skills. They both knew he would never be able to hold a job with his indifferent attitude.

"I can't just throw him out into the street," Shawna complained. "He is my flesh and blood. But he's ruining my life. I can't stand being around him. And, it's impossible to have a conversation with him."

"This is a unique problem, isn't it? He's not crazy enough to get him committed anywhere but he's not sane enough to live a normal life. It sure as hell doesn't seem fair that you're getting stuck with him for the rest of your life."

"Oh Jeff, don't say that! I can't take care of him forever. What about one of those half-way houses?"

"I don't know, but I think a social worker has to place people in those facilities. And have you ever seen one of those places? They're not pretty."

"I wonder what would happen if he didn't have me. He wouldn't be able to afford an apartment or even a room with no job."

"The street."

"Oh God, this is such an impossible quagmire. I guess I'll just have to go on like we are for the time being. Maybe something will come up that'll change the situation."

"Yeah, maybe so," he responded, but he could see no way out for her. If only her brother was normal… or completely disabled mentally so that he could be put away.

They spent Saturday hiking with Duffy in the hills behind Jeff's house. The weather was cold and breezy. A perfect day for mountaineering for Jeff would not take Duffy into the wilderness on a hot day. There were hundreds of snakes in those hills and Duffy was a very curious little dog.

On Sunday morning, they met Kevin at the Encino Golf Course in the valley. Jeff and Kevin played while Shawna rode along in the cart. At each tee box, the three of them resumed their discussion about the wayward brother. They all went out to Pedro's for dinner, then Shawna went home.

On the Wednesday evening news, it was reported that there had been yet another slaying in the same vain as the first two. It appeared that they had a serial killer on their hands. They also reported that they now had a DNA readout on the killer, but that there was no match with any previous arrestees in their databanks. The report went on to say that the victims' bodies were wrapped in dark colored blankets, then dumped. The detectives speculated that the killer used the blankets to prevent bloodstains in his vehicle. The weapon with which he had done the killing had not been found. Shawna began to shake with fear. She ran downstairs and sat in her car to call Jeff on her cell phone. She did not want to take any chances on being overheard.

"Jeff!"

"Honey, what is it?"

"I just saw the news. That serial killer struck again last weekend. Oh God Jeff, every time I'm gone, there's a murder. When I'm home, there are no murders. And the bodies are wrapped in blankets... dark blankets!"

"Shit. If you're tryin' to freak me out, it's working."

"I haven't been able to say this aloud, but I think maybe Jared's doing these things."

"I think we should call the police. Tell 'em what we suspect."

"Do you think I should?"

"Yeah, I do," he said. "If it's him, they need to stop him before he hurts someone else."

"I'll call right now, then I'll call you back."

"Okay."

She called information for the number of the local police station and had them ring her through. The phone was answered,

"Van Nuys division. How may I direct your call?"

"I have some information to give you about the serial killer that's been in the San Fernando Valley."

With no emotion and an irritatingly matter-of-fact attitude, the lady replied, "Hold on, I'll connect you with a detective."

While Shawna was holding for what seemed like forever, she thought to herself, "I have what might be critical information about the killer and they're moving like a bunch of slugs."

Finally, a man's voice came on the line, "I'll take your report, Miss."

"Officer, I have some information about the killer for you. I think it's my brother. Every time I'm gone, there's a new murder. When I'm home, nothing happens. He has the sickest pornography you've ever seen in his room and there are new baseball bats in his closet and stacks of blankets. He's always been really strange… antisocial… you know. And he can't hold a job for even a week."

"Your name?"

"Shawna Reese. His name is Jared Michael Reese."

"Address?"

"2075 Collins Avenue, Reseda," she replied in a frenzy.

"Home phone number?" She gave it to him.

"Aren't you gonna arrest him or take him in for questioning? Don't tell him I reported him. Can you make up some story about how you got the tip? Maybe some eye witness or something."

"Miss, I'll be candid with you. We've had hundreds of these reports—people so sure it's a relative of theirs or their next-door neighbor. A few things about the crimes match the comings and goings of someone they know and their imaginations run wild. We already have a suspect in these murders and we're pulling out all the stops to apprehend him. We'll keep your information on file. If the investigation leads us in that direction, we'll be sure to follow up."

"But… but… I feel so certain that it's him," she pleaded.

"You and about five hundred others. We'll call if we have any questions."

"Did you get all of the information? About the porno and the bats and the blankets?"

"It's all in the report," he said, sounding as if he had heard this exact story until he could barely stay awake through the conversation. "Thank you for your report," he stated dryly, then hung up.

She dialed Jeff's number immediately. "Honey, they won't do a thing to help us. The detective told me that hundreds of people are calling in with basically the same account."

"So they pretty much blew you off, huh?"

"No pretty much about it. He blew me off like I was some kinda' hysterical mental case. But now that I stop to think about it, it's probably pretty common for teenage boys to have girlie magazines and bats and blankets in their bedrooms, isn't it?"

"Yeah," Jeff chuckled. "That kinda' does sound like a million other boys. Well then, we'll have to conduct our own investigation. How about if you tell Jared you're staying with me next week end, then we'll follow him?"

"Yeah. That sounds like a good plan, but what do we do if we catch him trying to attack someone?" she asked.

Another golden opportunity had just presented itself to him. "God, you're right. I just wish we had a gun right now. Do you know anyone who has one?"

"Me! That's who! We can take my gun."

Walla! She took the bait. "What are you doing with a gun?"

"Oh, I had something happen once… a long time ago. No big deal, but it scared me so I got a permit and bought a Berretta 22."

"What happened?"

"I'll tell you about it sometime. Not right now. I'm too panicky about what's going on with Jared."

"Okay. Later then. But, I really want to know, Shawna."

"I'll come over to your house Saturday morning," she stated, ignoring his curiosity. "Do you think we need to stake him out all day or just in the evening?"

"I don't know. Maybe we should start in the afternoon. That way we'll be sure not to miss him."

CHAPTER 21

That Saturday morning, Shawna knocked on Jeff's door. She had been careful to be business as usual with Jared all week. She did not think he suspected anything. It appeared that he did not detect anything amiss in his room either. They must have put everything back just the way he had it—either that or he was too brain dead to notice.

Jeff had borrowed a company car so that Jared would not recognize it. He might have seen Jeff's at some point and that would put them at a disadvantage.

"Are you ready to become a sleuth?" he asked her.

"I guess. I'm so scared about what we might find out. God, I hope it's not Jared."

"Me too. But we need to be sure. The police aren't gonna be of any assistance until we have solid evidence to give them. Now, we're just a couple of alarmists."

"No. The detective said they already have a suspect."

"They do? Did he tell you who?"

"No," she told him. "He just said that they're putting all of their time and manpower on a particular suspect."

"Well, that's a relief. They must be pretty sure about this guy or they wouldn't waist their time. But let's still check up on Jared—just to ease our minds."

Jeff handed Shawna a baseball cap and then put one on himself. She tucked all of her hair up underneath. They also both wore shades. Hopefully, they would not be recognized. Jeff pulled the brown, 1999 Buick up to where they had a good view of Jared's Honda parked in the carport. He had picked the vehicle that he thought had the lowest profile. He was actually eligible for a company car, but he declined, having no need with the car he owned. When he asked permission to take a car, his boss said, "Anytime, any car. Just pick one and the garage attendant will sign you out and give you the keys." Nice place—great job.

They sat for two hours talking about Jared and what they would do if he were the one. They also talked about what they were going to do if he were not the one. They both agreed that they had to get him some serious help. It seemed that he had a hard-wired compulsion for deviant pornography. Shawna swore she did not know from where he could have gotten this deranged obsession. She told Jeff how wonderful and loving her parents had always been. How they did everything they could for the children. Their kids were their whole lives. She did admit; however, that they may have been a bit lax in the disciplinary department.

"Wait... there he is." Jeff interrupted. "He's getting into the car."

"Should I duck down?"

"Yeah, maybe you should, just until he gets going."

Jeff pulled out following Jared's car, being careful to keep a two-car distance. Jared made two left turns then pulled into a McDonald's about three miles from home. Again, Jeff pulled the car over to the curb and waited for the Accord to reappear on the other side of the drive through. Finally, he came out of the driveway and turned left onto the boulevard. Jeff resumed his pursuit. By this time, Shawna was sitting up in her seat. They followed Jared to a hardware store where he pulled in and parked near the entrance. They waited. He came out with a medium sized bag, then got back into his car and drove home.

"Well, he was hungry so he went to get some lunch. But I'd love to know what's in that bag."

Again, they parked alongside the road where they could see his car in the parking stall.

"God, honey, I wish we'd driven through McDonald's too. I'm hungry." Shawna announced.

"Me too and I have to pee. How about you?"

"Desperately!"

"What do you say we get some food? Back to McDonald's?"

"Amen to that. Let's go inside so we can use the potty. How do investigators do this?"

"For sure, I don't know. But he probably won't come out for a while. He'll be chomping down his happy meal. We'll come right back."

"Let's go."

They had something to eat and used the facilities at the same restaurant where Jared had gone. By the time they walked back out to their car, it was dark. They drove back to the apartment to find Jared's car gone.

"Oh shit! We missed him! We duck out for thirty minutes and he's gone."

"That'll teach us. Next time we bring food and a bottle to pee in," Shawna replied. They drove back to Jeff's house both feeling like they had a lot to learn about this stakeout business. You don't divert your eyes for one minute.

The next week, the news reported another murder—same MO; however, this young lady did not appear to have been sexually assaulted. It happened on Saturday night sometime. The same night they had let Jared get away from them. This one was thrown into a dumpster behind a strip mall—beaten and strangled. They both felt somehow responsible for this killing. If only they had not indulged their food cravings, maybe some young girl would still have her life in front of her.

CHAPTER 22

Christmas had crept up on them before they knew it. Jeff thought it might be just what the doctor ordered for the three of them to spend the holiday with his crazy (but normal for the most part) family. He invited Shawna to join him and she eagerly accepted. He made sure to include Jared. Shawna said that she would work on him. She too, thought it would be good for him to see a regular, loving family celebrating the holiday together.

"Jared, Jeff has invited us to his family's house for Christmas. I really want you to come."

It already sounded like an order to Jared. "I don't want to be around a bunch a' strange people," he protested.

"You haven't been around many normal families, Jared. Even if you don't want to talk, I think it would be eye opening for you to see how they interact with each other. I'll tell them that you're very shy. They won't be expecting anything from you. You don't have to perform. Okay?"

"You tryin' to be my shrink or what? The answer is no, I don't wanna go."

"Please Jared! For me? You don't have to talk at all."

"Damn it, Shawn, you never stop badgering me! If it's not one thing, it's something else! I just wanna be left alone."

"To lock yourself up in that room all day? Say yes, Jared—just this once. I'll take you home if you feel uncomfortable. Promise!"

"Shit!" He walked back into his room shaking his head.

On Christmas morning, Shawna helped Jared get dressed and comb his hair. He had already had one visit with her dentist where they started on the humungous job of cleaning the crusts of tarter off his teeth. They said it would take, at least, two more sessions to get them clean and after that, they suggested a whitening program, but at least they looked a little better than they had before. At least they didn't look like one, solid unit. She had forced him to take a shower, then when he came out for inspection, she sent him back a second time. After her eagle eye had groomed him to the hilt and she had given him the sniff test, they were off to Jeff's family's house for Christmas dinner.

When she rang the doorbell, Jeff made sure he was the one to answer. He hugged Shawna, then gave Jared a hug. A hug that was completely unresponded to, with arms that hung limply at his sides. He then introduced a multitude of family members and tried to include him in every conversation. He was always so clever at pulling teenagers out of their shells, but Jared was a stubborn case indeed. The boy hung his head and made one or two word answers to every question. Jeff and Shawna exhausted themselves in their attempts to draw him out. "I feel like I'm jumping through circus hoops for him," Jeff groaned into her ear.

They again sat at the table of honor with Jeff's parents, grandparents and his sister, Janice and her husband, Stan. Everyone immediately sensed Jared's problems and tried desperately to engage him in conversation. He answered all of them with his typical blank responses—answers so clipped that he appeared to be snotting them off. Finally, they gave up and began their usual family banter.

"Hector, you look so stylish in your suspenders," Shawna raved. She thought he really looked cute in his pale blue shirt with royal blue and white suspenders.

"I don't have any hips. If I don't wear 'em, my pants keep fallin' down. Agnes buys 'em for me. A pair to go with every shirt color. Pretty dapper, huh?" he chuckled as he ran his thumbs up and down the inside of his straps.

"Very well turned out," she teased.

Roast turkey with all of the trimmings was again severed. The mouth-watering courses started making their way around the table on platters and in serving bowls.

"I can't get comfortable in this damn chair... with this arthritis in every part of my body, especially my back," Hector started in. "I didn't git three winks sleep last night. Up every half hour tryin' to squeeze the piss out with this misery in my prostate!"

"Hector, can we get through one dinner without being given a mental image of your bathroom habits?" Jeff snapped.

"He kept wakin' me up out of a sound sleep—jumpin' up and down and up and down," his wife, Agnes added. "And every time he came back to bed, he had to announce exactly how much came out—'three lousy squirts,' he'd say." Agnes kept wiping her nose with a hanky she was keeping in her lap. She looked up and addressed herself to Shawna, "My nose runs all the time... all the time."

"Do you have allergies?" Shawna asked with sincere concern.

"I'm allergic to everything!"

"I surrender," Jeff said as he rolled his eyes and shrugged his shoulders to Shawna. She giggled out loud. How terribly wonderful to have a solidly normal family. She adored Jeff's family.

"So Stan, what's a good program for getting my finances in order?" Ray, Jeff's father, asked. Stan was a systems analyst with a major bank chain so everyone enjoyed picking his brain regarding his or her computer needs.

"What exactly do you need, just household records or do you want something that can handle investments? There're some real good programs out now."

"Oh no, are we gonna talk about computers through the whole dinner?" Janice chimed in.

"What do you wanna talk about… ironing?" Stan shot back.

"There's a big sale at Macy's," Janice said to Shawna in an attempt to compete with the men's topic.

Shawna found it hilarious and joined right in with the women against the men competition. "Yeah, I went crazy in ladies foundations."

"Not to mention the great deals on teddies and baby doll nighties," Debbie added.

Agnes was eager to put her two cents in, "I got myself one of those thong bikini's."

Not catching on to the joke, Hector flashed his wife a look of open-mouthed shock. The entire table started battling with the men now talking football and the women talking cooking and baking…each sex trying to out shout the other. Everyone ended up in sidesplitting laughter. Everyone, that is, except Jared. He sat stone-faced throughout the entire dinner.

After the meal, Shawna jumped up to help clear the table. She was now feeling so very comfortable with Jeff's relatives. Everyone was getting up from their tables and mixing and talking and laughing. The sound of children playing, screaming and crying was actually comforting to her. Such a huge group of animated people—a typical large family.

After helping with the clean up, Shawna joined Jeff in the den where he was sitting with some of his siblings and their little ones. Jared sat off in a corner, refusing to interact with the family. At one point, one of Jeff's little nieces approached him and asked him to play "Candyland" with her. Jared's answer was "I don't know that game," then he got up to use the bathroom.

"I'll play," Shawna said. A delighted little girl brought her game over to teach Shawna the rules.

She glanced over at Jeff at intervals to see a cluster of small children clamoring for his attention. He may not have much patience with children, but they sure love him, she thought to herself. She watched them pulling at his pant legs and climbing all over him. All of a sudden, a little blonde-haired girl dumped her pumpkin pie with whipped cream faced down into his lap. Jeff instantly jumped up to brush the pie back onto its paper plate while one of his sisters ran to get a damp towel to sponge the gooey mess off his trousers. The little girl immediately broke into shrieks of frustration that she had lost her precious piece of pie. Shawna's stomach ached from belly laughing. Jeff did not appear to share in everyone's amusement over the episode.

The family had drawn names for their gift exchange. It would have sent anyone to the poor house to buy presents for each family member. It was so festive with everyone talking, laughing and exclaiming over gifts. And the house was decorated to the max—overdone really, but Shawna loved it. Finally, Jeff handed Shawna a small, beautifully wrapped box. She opened it to discover the most gorgeous diamond drop earrings she had ever seen.

"Oh Jeff! They're stunning! You spent way too much money!"

"I did? Then I'd better take them back."

"No," she said in a baby voice as she clutched the box to her heart. Everyone laughed.

She had given Jeff a pair of German antique candleholders that he had raved about on one of their antiquing excursions. She went back the next day to make the purchase. He was more than thrilled that she had taken notice and kept them for his Christmas present. She had also bought Duffy some bones and a fuzzy squeaky toy.

Jared did not take part in the gift exchange. He was now out on the back patio, smoking one cigarette after another—something he did when he felt ill at ease. Jeff and his parents had gifts for him, but gave them to Shawna to take home. They all gave her looks of sincere understanding.

After about two hours, she told Jeff that she'd better get the "stick in the mud" home. She said her goodbyes to all and thanked them profusely for their most gracious hospitality. Jared did say thank you with the coaxing of a firm elbow in his side. Jeff asked her to call him so that he would know she and Jared had gotten home safely.

CHAPTER 23

On the following Wednesday, after Jeff got home from work, he decided to probe through some of the boxes that were being stored in his garage. Perhaps Mrs. Reese had some medical or psychological information among her important papers… something that might shine a little more light on Jared's odd deportment.

He went through the stacks of boxes until he found two that Shawna had labeled "MOM'S IMPORTANT PAPERS." He carefully opened the first box with a sharp knife cutting along the tape that held the cardboard flaps closed. He pulled out folders that were labeled tax returns, insurance policies, property info. He taped that box back up and opened the next one. Out of this box, he pulled folders that had "MEDICAL RECORDS" written on them. He sat down on the garage floor as he opened the first one and found some of Jared's medical files. A thorough perusal of the papers revealed that he had been diagnosed with several emotional disorders back in 1996, when he was just ten years old. Antisocial and schizoid personality disorders were listed.

Further investigation revealed files that diagnosed sociopathic tendencies, lack of empathy with others, little or no eye contact, non-compliant behavior and a propensity for aggressive and violent acting out.

"So his parents did have some idea of how deeply entrenched his problems were," he voiced out loud. He read about sessions with psychiatrists that exposed the depth of their concern about his mental instability. He saw notes that said, "Loner, does not 'fit in' with other children. Prefers to remain isolated from society. Lives inside his fantasies—resulting in an inability to form real life attachments. Could be a future threat to society. May be dangerous to women. Anti-social problems could lead to psychotic behavior."

He bundled the files up in a large rubber band planning to show Shawna as soon as possible. Then a file entitled, "MEDICAL RECORDS, SHAWNA" caught his eye. Of course he was unable to stop himself from tearing open the seal and pulling out the contents. He started sifting through the papers.

Only one file flagged him. It was a report from a gynecologist—a Doctor Neil Grisham who had done a procedure called *hymenorraphy* on her. He did not understand the medical terminology, but he clearly read, "vaginal reconstruction, replacement of hymen." It was dated March 4, 1994. He felt the sharp sting of betrayal stabbing through his body.

"How could she lie to me like this?" he bellowed. "What kind of stupid chump am I, anyway? I loved her. I trusted her and believed what she told me. Why the fuck is she lying about being a virgin. About me being her first experience. Is this some little game she thinks is funny? I've been had. She's as sick as her moron brother."

He did not move from the garage floor for some time. Thoughts were swimming through his head as he tried to make sense of this humungous lie he had been told. Finally, he staggered to his feet and went into the house to call Kevin.

"Hello."

"Kevin? It's Jeff."

"What's wrong? You sound awful!"

"I've never felt worse in my whole united life."

"Hey, pal, this is serious?"

"It is."

"You got something on Jared?" Kevin was almost afraid to hear the answer.

"No. On Shawna."

"Jesus Jeff, do you want to talk about this on the phone?"

"No, but I need to talk to you. Can you meet me after work tomorrow night?"

"Of course I can, buddy. Are you gonna be all right till then? I've never heard you sound so down."

"I can hang in 'til tomorrow. Maybe together, we can make some sense of this. Meet you at Pedro's at six?"

"I'll be there. But Jeff, call me tonight if you need to talk, okay?"

"Okay. You're a real friend, Kev."

CHAPTER 24

Jeff was already waiting when Kevin arrived at Pedro's. He waved him down from a booth across the restaurant. Kevin slid in on the opposite side and was shocked by his friend's appearance. He looked as if he had not slept and Kevin noticed something even more unusual. His eyes looked as if he had been crying.

"I've been worried about you all night. What in the world is this thing you found out about Shawna?"

"I opened some of the boxes she had stored in my garage to see if there was any medical or whatever information about Jared."

"Snooping? Again? When has that nose of yours ever done anything but cause you grief?"

"But Kev, look what I found this time," he said as he shoved the medical record across the table for Kevin to view.

His buddy studied the paper for a few minutes while Jeff sat awaiting his response. Finally, he looked up. "She had some kind of procedure done to make it seem like she's a virgin," Kevin said. "I've heard of this. Girls in the Middle East get this done so that they can get a man to marry them. A lot of men over there insist on their wives being virgins. But why would Shawna do this? It doesn't make sense."

"She lied. She tricked me. Made a damn fool outta me."

"No. I don't think she was trying to do any such thing. It

says here that she had it done in 1994. That would have made her twenty-two."

"Maybe she was real promiscuous before that," Jeff blurted. "A hooker or something."

"Shawna? Get serious! I've gotten to know her so much better now and I can tell she's a real class act."

"Well, whatever her reasons, she lied to me again. She's a fucking liar, Kev! I can't take any more of this shit. Her sinister brother was bad enough. Now I find out that she's nuts too. All I ever wanted was to have peace and quiet. An easy, simple life with no chaos. Look what I get."

"You know you have to confront her about your findings, don't you?"

"I don't have the energy to fight this anymore. It's one mystery after another with this girl. I wouldn't believe a word she said if she were sitting on a stack of Bibles. She's lost my trust for good now."

He gazed into Kevin's eyes and saw a straightforward expression. Something that was entirely out of character for him. "You told me you love her. You can't just take a powder without talking this out. She owes you an explanation. You owe her a chance to clarify her side."

"I need a few days to think things through."

"That didn't help last time and it won't help this time. It's just gonna fester until you confront her. Are you gonna call?"

"Okay."

"You mean it?"

"Yeah."

They ate their dinner discussing all of the "what if's" they could muster up. When they got up to leave, Jeff said, "Thanks Kev. I don't know what I'd do without you."

"You don't have to get all mushy on me...just call her. Then tell me everything that was said." They both laughed, then gave each other a big, bear hug.

Jeff felt a little guilty for going back on his promise to call Shawna, but he just was not ready to have it out with her. She called him at work several times, but he told Ginny to take a message. He desperately missed her, but he was seething with anger at this colossal betrayal. How, in God's name, could she explain her way out of this hoodwink?

He slept in on Saturday morning, mostly due to a deep depression. At around noon, the doorbell rang. He slipped into his robe and walked out through the living room. He opened the door to see Shawna standing there. He had figured it might be her.

"Why the hell are you avoiding me, Jeff?"

Without inviting her in, he stood staring into her eyes as a hush of silence hung between them.

"What is wrong with you?" she demanded. He still did not move or speak.

She grabbed him by his shoulders and shook him as hard as she could.

"I want you to leave," he spoke with ice in his voice.

"Is this your way of dumping girls? What the hell did I do? Is it because of Jared? I can't help it if I was stuck with a fruitcake for a brother!"

All of a sudden, he snapped. He yanked her into the house by her arm pushing her towards the couch and shoving her down into a sitting position.

"You're gonna sit right there until you tell me everything!" he shouted. "And I have a feeling it's not gonna be a short story." He stomped into the bedroom and reappeared with the medical report. He threw it into her lap and exploded, "Explain this! And try the truth for a change!"

As Shawna examined the paper, her expression changed in an eerie sort of way. She sat silent with her eyes cast down, him watching her intently. He waited and waited for her response, but none was forthcoming.

Finally he spoke, "Tryin' to think up a good lie?"

She looked up into his face. "I had no idea my mother had saved this."

"Your mother? What does she have to do with this?"

"This was her idea. She urged me to get this done." She was speaking as though she had fallen into some kind of trance. There was no expression—no emotion. She sat paralyzed staring at the piece of paper—as if she were reading her own obituary.

"Shawna!" he barked. "Snap out of it and talk to me! You owe me an explanation for this. Tell me why you had this done—why you lied to me. I'm goddamned sick of these lies!"

She looked up at him through glazed eyes.

"Jared's not my brother… he's my son."

Jeff fell backwards onto the love seat as his head began to spin out of control. He could feel his heart pounding wildly in his chest.

Shawna sat with her eyes fixed on him, then she began to come out of her trance-like state. She walked over and sat down next to him.

"That's the last thing I expected to hear," he spoke with a raspy voice. He placed his arms around her body and they sat holding one another for a long, long time. When his breathing again became normal, he asked, "Do you want to tell me the story? From the beginning?"

"I've never told anyone this before. Never discussed it once."

"Does Jared know…that you're his mother?"

"No."

"This is gonna be a horror story, isn't it?"

"Yes," she said, then began her saga:

"When I was thirteen, there was a prolific serial killer terrorizing Oregon. Most of the murders were upstate, but he seemed to have no pattern. Bodies were found all over the state…

all the same MO. Young girls raped and beaten to death with a heavy lead pipe.

"One afternoon, I was on my way home from school. It was a two-mile walk and I had just started out. A man pulled up beside me—seemed frantic. He shouted, 'Your house is on fire. Your mother sent me to get you. Jump in quick!'

"Without one thought, I leaped into his car. All I could think of was my mom and dad maybe being burned to death—and our house burning to the ground. He peeled out fast and I started blasting questions at him… like 'Are my parents hurt,' and 'Is it real bad, the fire?' He didn't answer me. Then he turned down a little used road and I said, 'This is the wrong way. You need to go back to the main street.' He still said nothing.

"That's when it dawned on me that he wasn't driving me home. I said, 'There's no fire at my house, is there?' He turned to me and I stared into a face of pure evil. I hadn't really looked at him until then. I tried to jump out of the car even though he was driving fast. There was nothing there—no door handle, no window crank, no way out."

She looked at Jeff and saw that his eyes were wide with horror. "Should I continue?"

"Please." His voice cracked and he tightened his arm around her waist. Her body was shuddering as she picked up where she had left off.

"He drove till the road came to a dead end, then he turned off the engine. I asked him what he was gonna do to me. He didn't answer. He jerked my hands behind my back and tied them together so tight I yelled out. Then he yanked me out of the driver's side door and dragged me for a long way into the woods. I started to scream at the top of my lungs, then he punched me so hard I all but passed out.

"He threw me down in the dirt and tore off my clothes. Everything. Then he raped me. It hurt so bad I couldn't stop screaming. He kept punching me to shut me up. When he was done, he picked up his lead pipe and brought it down hard on my chest. He looked like a madman who had flipped into a wild rage. He started beating me harder and harder—smashing the pipe down on my legs, my arms, my head. I heard my own voice screaming bloody murder. Then I blacked out.

"The next thing I remember was opening my eyes in the hospital. There was a tube going down my throat so I couldn't talk. I just kept passing out from the pain. I remember seeing my parents' faces—looking frantic. Every time I opened my eyes, either my mother or father was sitting next to my bed, holding my hand. I had sustained numerous broken bones, a skull fracture, a ruptured spleen and massive internal bleeding. It was a miracle that I lived.

"Two hikers had heard my screams and found me almost beaten to death. The killer was so caught up in what he was doing to me he didn't hear them approach. They grabbed him off of me and beat him senseless. They tied him up real good—to a tree, I think. They left him there in the woods, then they carried me back to where their car was parked and drove me straight to the hospital in town—giving me C.P.R. all the way. They called the police from the hospital and told them what happened and where to find the perpetrator."

Jeff's face went pallid. "God, Shawna, I feel like such a stupid jerk! They caught him, then?"

"Yes. The two men were more than glad to identify him and testify at the trial. I was in critical condition and couldn't go to court. The detectives brought me pictures so that I could point him out and they took semen samples from me when I first arrived at the hospital. It turned out that he was the serial killer that had raped and murdered over twenty girls in a two-year span. He's serving a life sentence at the Oregon State Penitentiary now—a maximum security prison."

Shawna took a few deep breaths, then went on, "I was in the hospital for months. It didn't even occur to anyone that I was missing my periods. The trauma to my body was so severe, that menses probably would have stopped anyway. I was five months pregnant before we started to suspect anything. By that time, it was too late to terminate the pregnancy. They have methods now, but back then, they didn't.

"My mother decided to keep my baby. She said it was our flesh and blood and she and dad would raise it as if it were their own.

"So Jared was brought up as my little brother. From the beginning, I only thought of him as my sibling—never as my own child. I was just a kid myself!

"Nothing was ever said about my attack. My parents thought that it was best to put it all behind us as if it had never happened." She looked into Jeff's puffy, red eyes, "But it did happen, Jeff and it's haunted me ever since. I've constructed my whole life around a lie. That sickening, nagging fear of being found out has been with me every single second. That's why I never dated. I just couldn't. And anyway, I've been petrified for all these years to trust any man with my heart or my body."

"You poor baby!" Jeff cried.

"My parents were getting worried about me cause I never, ever had a boyfriend or even a date. So when I was twenty-two, mom begged me to have that surgery so that I could have my innocence back—a new beginning, she must've hoped. This was to give me back my virginity that had been ripped away through no fault of my own. I did it to please her, but I had no intentions of allowing any man to come near me. And I never did until I met you that night at the company party."

"How... why did you give me a chance?" he asked.

"I don't know. You seemed so very different than any man I had ever met. So nice. So sincere. I was terrified, but I really, really wanted to let you in. So, you see, Jeff, you really were my first love."

They were both quivering in shock—Jeff from hearing the worst thing he had ever heard in his life... Shawna from addressing her nightmare for the very first time. "Honey, you mean to tell me you never received any therapy at all to get you through this devastating experience?"

"None. My parents brushed it under the rug. I guess they thought I'd forget about it in time. That if we never talked about it, it would be as though it never happened," she spoke with great difficulty. Then, suddenly, she began exploding into wails of anguish. She had not allowed herself to reconstruct the hideousness of that day until this very moment. Only flashes here and there would assault her awareness—mental pictures that she struggled desperately on a daily basis to push down.

The floodgates burst open and she rolled onto the floor in absolute hysteria. Jeff lay down next to her and held her close as she sobbed.

"Just let it all out, sweetheart. Don't hold anything back. Let it purge. My poor darling, stuffing this inside for all these years."

They lay on the carpet for hours. Occasionally, she would begin to quiet, just to break, again, into wild shrieking, pounding her fists on the floor—Jeff repeating "Let it out, honey—feed into it, if you can."

It was six o'clock in the evening when she finally settled down. Then, she began breathing deeply… relaxing her body into Jeff's embrace. "Are you hungry? Do you want something to eat?"

"Yes," she replied through a hoarse voice.

"Okay," he managed a smile. "Shall I call for a pizza?"

She nodded.

He pulled a handkerchief out of his robe pocket and handed it to her. "It might have a few bad spots on it," he warned her. She smiled back at him as she blew her nose into the white cloth.

CHAPTER 25

They ate their pizza at the kitchen table while Shawna began talking in depth about her ordeal for the first time. She spoke about every feeling she was experiencing throughout the entire kidnapping and attack. She told him about how much pain she suffered in the subsequent months. Then to be hit with the horrendous news that she was expecting that monster's baby. The way her parents tried to pretend that it never really happened. Calling Jared their little "oops baby." Making believe that he was their blessed accident.

Jeff sat listening intently, asking questions here and there. They talked into the night, then they got into Jeff's bed and cuddled close. "God, I want to hold you and never let go," he whispered in her ear. "I swear I'll never doubt you again. We're gonna get you into therapy right away, honey. I have a great psychologist. He helped get me through all of my childhood anger and resentment. I know he can help you, too. I'll call him on Monday, okay?"

"Okay. Thank you for taking care of me, Jeff."

"I'm gonna take such good care of you, honey. I love you beyond words."

"I love you, too."

She quickly fell into a sound sleep but Jeff lay awake holding her—rehashing her gruesome ordeal over and over in his head. Putting himself in her place, thinking of how completely helpless she was. Imagining how excruciating it was every time a thunderous blow from that lead pipe came down on her body. Knowing that she was going to die at the hands of another human being—if indeed he could even be considered one. Finally, sleep descended upon him and they slept for twelve hours locked in each other's arms.

Jeff was awakened by Duffy's wet nose pushing against his face. The little dog was hungry. The insanity of the previous day had completely diverted Jeff's attention and Duffy had missed both his morning and evening meals. Jeff opened his eyes slowly to see an adorable, whiskered muzzle nudging him in an attempt to get some attention. "Oh, Duffy, you poor little guy. I forgot to feed you yesterday."

He looked over to see Shawna smiling. "Oh no," she said. "He needs something to eat, right away."

"Good morning," he greeted.

"Good morning. Thank you so much for being there for me last night. I'm glad you found that paper. It forced the issue and that's just what I needed in order to break free."

"You feel better, sweetheart?"

"Oh God, better than I've felt since before it happened."

Jeff kissed her lips then got out of bed and put his robe on. "Would you have told me about it eventually?"

"I think so. It's just that I had buried it so deeply inside. That lie had long since become a part of who I was. Sometimes I actually thought it never happened. That Jared was, indeed, my little brother. But the ugly feeling in the pit of my stomach was always there. It never left me for even a minute…until now."

Jeff gave her a tender smile. "I'm so glad it's all out in the open. You sleep some more, honey. I'll go feed this poor, starving creature and I'll fix you breakfast. How about we eat it in here so we can just veg out today? Sound okay?"

"Sounds perfect."

When he came back with the breakfast trays, Shawna had already gotten up to shower and brush her teeth. She had put on one of Jeff's big T-shirts and scooted back into bed, under the covers.

"Cheese and mushroom omelets," he announced.

"Wow, that looks scrumptious."

"I feel just awful about the way I treated you. Jumping to conclusions like that."

"No. You had every right to think the worst. It looked like I was trying to pull a fast one on you. You didn't know. That day when you grabbed my driver's license, I all but had a nervous breakdown. It really put me on the spot for the first time. The only explanation that popped into my head was that I didn't want you to know that I was thirty one and still a virgin."

"Well, you weren't lying. You were thirty-one and still a virgin. What he did to you did not alter that fact in my mind." She smiled at him through hazy eyes.

When they finished breakfast, Jeff told her that he had been looking through her mother's boxes in order to find anything of interest about Jared. He brought the medical file to her and pointed out what he had found. He read the psychological profile and the medical test results to her.

"Have you ever heard of schizoid personality disorder?" he asked.

"No. Mom kept all of his therapy and medical information a secret from me. What is it?"

"I think it's a condition that causes the patient to disconnect from people and society. They isolate themselves and become entirely obsessed with their own thoughts and fantasies. They display peculiar behavior."

"Boy, that's Jared, isn't it?"

"Yeah. Your parents must have known a lot more about him than they ever let on. There are stacks of reports. I was going to read them all, but I got sidetracked by your folder."

She laughed. It was good to hear her laugh again. They studied all of Jared's records and learned that doctor after doctor had diagnosed him with mental, emotional and social problems. The doctors all considered the possibility that these conditions may have been inherited from the father.

"Jeff, I want to find out if his biological father has the same mental illnesses. And what his childhood was like. It seems like Jared might be a 'chip off the old block.' He sure looks like him from what I can remember."

"Do you think the prison will release his medical records to you?"

"I want to go there. We can talk to the prison doctor. And Jeff…I want to see him. I want to confront the man who meant to kill me."

"You do? What are you gonna say to him?"

"I don't know. Maybe nothing. Maybe I just want to look into his evil eyes one more time. See this monster behind bars where he can't ever hurt me again."

"I'll go with you."

"You didn't expect me to go without you, did you?"

"I hoped not," he said. "When do you want to go?"

"Want to fly up next weekend?"

"Okay. This is gonna be some confrontation. Are you sure you're up to this?"

"I have to see him. It'll give me closure. I want to find out what his family was like and I want to see how much Jared is like him."

They agreed to fly to Salem, Oregon the next weekend. Then, the following weekend, they would resume their surveillance on Jared. Shawna had apprised Jeff that there had indeed been another killing in the same mode last Saturday night. The night they had let Jared slip away.

CHAPTER 26

Jeff had completed his basketball return gadget and was deeply engaged in a new project at work. His Basketball Boomerang had passed the company's kid test, but for whatever reason, it wasn't moving off the store shelves. No one knew why this happened sometimes, but it was time to put this disappointment aside and give his full attention to his current endeavor. He was now creating a baby doll that looked and felt so real, only very close inspection revealed it to be a toy. He had completed the prototype and it had passed the child test as a mashing success. The company loved the doll and immediately set into motion the production of numerous accessories to be purchased along with baby.

He was glad to be busy for the upcoming scene with Shawna's assailant was not something to which he was looking forward. But he was determined to be there with her to lend moral (and physical) support.

Shawna's workweek was equally strained with nightmares every night and fear of facing this fiend permeating her every waking thought. What would he be like? What would he say to her? Would he be remorseful? She had to prepare herself for the worst-case scenario. He may be harboring hatred for her for being the one who finally got him locked up. But she had to know.

Jeff called her that next Thursday and suggested that they disable Jared's car. He and Kevin would sneak over on Friday night to do the deed. This would render him helpless for the weekend. Shawna was impressed that he had come up with such a brilliant scheme. She too, had been worried sick about leaving him to perhaps add another victim to his fast growing list. That was, of course, if he were the notorious "Saturday Night Killer."

Before she went to bed on Friday night, she told Jared that she and Jeff were going to Palm Springs for a little "get away" and that she had to leave very early in the morning.

They landed at the Salem Airport at 12:40 PM on Saturday, then rented a Ford Mustang for the trip to the Oregon State Penitentiary. "2605 State Street," Shawna said as she read Jeff the directions from the map they had faxed to her. She had called from work during the week and spoken with the superintendent. He was very sympathetic to her case and told her that the prison doctor would be more than happy to accommodate her needs and wants. He also informed her that she could, indeed, schedule a visit with Ivan Lee Adler if she so chose.

"I remember your case well," John Ross, the superintendent said as he greeted the couple. "You are one lucky girl to be standing here, Miss Reese. He's a killing machine without a shred of conscience. One of our most violent inmates to date."

He took them to the office of the prison doctor, Doctor Henry Gilbert—a short, thin man who looked to be in his early sixties. The somber, blue eyes behind his wire rimmed glasses appeared laden with stress.

As they walked in, they were struck by how utilitarian the office was. Nothing fancy or expensive like one would see in an outside doctor's office. No interior designer's touch here. The desk, at which Doctor Gilbert sat, was gray metal and the chairs were made of cheap wood with coffee-colored Naugahyde covering the seats. The bookshelves were metal racks bracketed to the walls. All of the furnishings were functional at best. Jeff immediately thought of a hundred ways this office could be spruced up with some color and a few decent pieces of art.

The doctor was anticipating their arrival and had Ivan Adler's file open on top of his desk. "So you think your son may have inherited some predilections from his biological father, huh?"

"I think so. Don't you think these tendencies could have been passed to his son?"

The doctor opted not to speculate about this. He simply shook his head and replied, "It's impossible to know. But we're learning so much nowadays about genetics and how much is passed along family lines."

"Anyway it might give me a clearer picture as to what Jared's problems may be. I realize you can't tell me everything in Ivan's medical files, but any information you can share will certainly be appreciated," Shawna said.

"Well, I can tell you that he has been analyzed by several psychiatrists and he has undergone numerous medical tests. Here, it says he was diagnosed with narcissistic and antisocial personality disorders soon after being incarcerated, but these are just a few of his problems. They are numerous." Shawna and Jeff looked at each other with grave expressions on their faces.

Doctor Gilbert continued. "He's schizoid which accounts for severe withdrawal—a cutting off from interaction with others, even family."

"Is that where they hear voices in their head?" Shawna inquired.

"No, that's schizophrenia you're thinking of. Schizoid conditions cause the patient to be detached, displaying signs of suspicion and mistrust of others. They're loners living in a self-made fantasy world—sometimes delusional. Show only a narrow range of feelings. Underachievers.

"Interviews with Ivan's relatives revealed that he had always been exceedingly withdrawn—even as a small child. Never had friends. Did poorly in school. Seemed detached from the rest of the world, spending all his time secluded from the rest of the family. Poor hygiene." The doctor looked up momentarily, "His teeth were rotting out of his head when he came here. Had to have three pulled and eleven root canals."

He shuffled through more papers, then resumed his report. "Violent tendencies began to surface in his early adolescence. There were two murders of young girls, nine and eleven in his neighborhood that were never solved. It's now believed that these were two of his early victims. When questioned, he says he can't remember back that far." He looked up at Jeff and Shawna. "I guess because there were so many. Says here that he has an uncle who was arrested on three different occasions for indecent exposure and lewd acts upon a minor."

He went on to read off more observations from the mental health staff. It seemed as if it were Jared's records being read. "Withdrawn, disconnected, filled with self hatred, no interest in social interaction, no eye contact, sociopathic, addicted to violent pornography, trouble obtaining and holding any type of employment.

"On going interviews with prison psychiatrists revealed that he would usually stake out a victim prior to abduction. He would observe her patterns of coming and going. He tried to select vics who appeared soft and vulnerable. Ones who wouldn't be able to put up much of a fight." He peered over his glasses at Shawna. "He also liked the pretty ones.

"He told doctors that sex was only part of it. His need to overpower and totally dominate his victim was what drove him. His words: 'It's like I owned the person. The murder was a sexual rush.' This need was so strong, he felt helpless to stop his behavior. It says he took a perverse pleasure in watching his victims as he inflicted torture on them. He was a ritualistic killer. He would always use the same pattern in his sexually motivated crimes. First he would render them defenseless, either by restraint or bodily injury, then he would rape them. After he finished, he would kill them. Then he would have post-mortem sex with them.

"When questioned about the first homicide he could recall, he answered, 'When I was around eighteen, I picked up this girl who was hitch-hikin'—couldn't a been more than twelve or thirteen. Anyway, I wanted to have sex with her, but she didn't want to—so I killed 'er'"

He flipped through the stacks of papers. "There's a lot more here, but it would take weeks to get through it all. Is there anything else you want to know?"

"You've given me so much that I need to know. Is there anything else about his family?"

Doctor Gilbert pulled out a folder that had "family history" written on the tab. "Well, let's see… yes, it says that the father was an alcoholic. He was killed in a car accident when Ivan was nineteen. He was driving drunk. The accident was his fault. No one else was killed.

"He still has a mother and a sister who come to visit every few months or so. I've interviewed them," he said looking up momentarily. "The mother is obese. Has a real hard time getting around. She seems a little odd. The sister still lives with mom. Never married." Then, glancing back down at the file, he continued, "The mother and father were not very involved with parenting him."

"Was he raised by someone else?" Shawna asked.

"No," the doctor replied. "They just weren't very good parents. They pretty much let him go and do as he pleased. No supervision to speak of."

"Enablers," Jeff interjected.

The doctor nodded. "I guess no one ever said 'no' to him. The family said that Ivan always seemed to amuse himself. Never had one friend—never wanted one. They said he was always off alone somewhere. Didn't even relate to the family. The mother stated that he 'Spent too much time locked up in that room of his.'" He looked up again. "I hope it helps you with your son. I'm truly sorry you have to go through this, Miss Reese. It should never have happened."

They thanked the doctor and went to the employee's cafeteria for some lunch. Then they had an appointment to visit with her would-be-killer.

Both of them were visibly shaken from the account of Ivan Lee Adler's condition. His personality traits were Jared all over again. Now, it was plain to Shawna that her son had inherited a lot of his strange behavior from his father. Had he inherited his father's diabolical taste for blood as well?

CHAPTER 27

The warden led them through some long; sterile looking hallways all painted pale gray, then he unlocked a large, steel door at the end of one of the corridors. They were ushered to an area where there were cubicles with thick glass separating the visitors from the inmates. Both of them were instructed to sit down in chairs and each to pick up one of the two phones that were indicated. They were to wait for Ivan Lee Adler to be brought to the other side of the glass by one of the guards. They waited.

Jeff took Shawna's hand in his and squeezed it. She squeezed back—hard. "There's never a dull moment with you," he said in a useless attempt to bring some normalcy to this chilling ordeal.

"Thank God you're here with me. I would never hold up through this alone. Look," she held her hand out. "I'm shaking."

"It's okay, honey," he reassured her. "He can't hurt you now." They sat, both frozen in grizzly anticipation—both with eyes glued to the door Ivan would be walking through at any moment.

Just then, the heavy, steel door slid open on the other side of the glass. A monster was escorted through by a strapping, young warden. His wrists and ankles were shackled so he walked with short, dragging steps. The first sight of him sent shock waves through Shawna's body. In a flash, she was back in that car looking into the face of a serial killer… her killer. Out of nowhere, her screams ricocheted off the walls of the acoustically live room.

Jeff grabbed her so she would not fall off of her seat. He could see that she was about three milliseconds from passing out. The attendant rushed up from where he was positioned behind the couple. "You okay? Do you want to go ahead with the visit?" he asked. She nodded.

The guard had halted Ivan's steps when he heard Shawna's wails. The two men stood awaiting further instructions. The attendant waved them forward and they, again, began the slow, hesitant steps towards the inmate's side of the cubicle.

His eyes were dark and cold. Eyes that seemed to look not out into the world around him, but inward—into the darkness of his own soul. His brows jutted out over his eyes with that same protruding ridge as Jared's. He was a big man and he now looked to be in his late forties. He shuffled to his chair giving Shawna the same vacant stare that had become so familiar to her. He appeared stone faced and unapproachable. The warden handed him the receiver and stood behind him. He held it to his ear and waited for Shawna to speak.

"Do... do you know who I am?" she asked in a voice that was steadier than she had anticipated.

"Yeah," he muttered in a deep, expressionless voice.

"I came here because I wanted some closure. I've never dealt with what you did to me. Also, I got pregnant as a result of your gruesome attack. My parents kept the baby and he's now seventeen."

"Yeah, I heard about it."

"I think he might be following in your footsteps. He has serious problems and I wanted to see what his biological father is like." With this, she burst into sobs. "The doctor told me a lot about your mental illnesses and it sounds so much like Jared," she choked out.

"Whatta you want?"

"I want you to know that you ruined my life! I've never gotten over the fear—the terror of that day. I was almost dead when those two heroic men came and saved me. Then, I was flat on my back in the hospital for months after your attack. When I woke up, there was a tube going down my throat and casts on both of my arms and my right leg. My chest was bond tight to stabilize my broken ribs…and my entire head was shaved and bandaged. Every part of my body was on fire with agonizing pain." She paused for a response but he sat there, in front of her eyes like a block of ice. "How could you do that to me? Rape me? Bludgeon me almost to death with that lead pipe. Have you ever given one thought to how you would like having that done to you?"

"No…can't say I have."

"Then you have absolutely no remorse for anyone you hurt or killed?"

"I wish I didn't have to do those things…but I do," he stated flatly.

"Why are you so compelled to hurt women? If you got out of here today, would you resume you old ways and go looking for a victim?"

"I gotta say if they hadn't caught me, I would've kept on. There was nothin' I could do to stop. When I'd git done with one, it would satisfy me for a time, then I'd git obsessed with huntin' for a new one. I couldn't git it outta my mind 'til I did it again. There's no way I'm gonna change till the day I die. I've killed a thousand times in my head since I been in here. You gotta understand, I wasn't thinkin' about them. I wanted to do it. It felt good to me."

"Do you have any feelings at all about what you did to me?"

"It wasn't nothin' personal. You were just there. I watched you for two weeks before I picked you up."

This last bit of information made her skin crawl. He had stalked his prey—planned his gruesome strategy for two weeks before he had surrendered to the demons in his mind. "Why me?" she asked with the hatred unmistakable in her voice. "Why did you pick me?"

"You were pretty, you know, like a trophy. And you looked trusting—easy to trap. Like you wouldn't put up too much of a fight."

Her head fell against Jeff's shoulder and the tears streamed down her cheeks. Her body convulsed in sobs as her mind traveled back to that horrific day. The way she jumped right into his car. The way she believed what he had told her. Her parents whom she loved so much were perhaps burned or dead. The house they had shared as a family was going up in flames. All she could think of was getting home as fast as she could. Home to her mom and dad.

Finally, she raised her eyes to gaze into her killer's face one last time. "Do you even care that you have a son?"

"If he's like me, I'm sorry for 'im. I'm a sick mother fucker."

"Can I ask you, were you heavily into pornography?"

"Since I was a kid. I lived it."

Shawna turned and looked at Jeff who was sitting with the phone to his ear, taking in the whole conversation. She shook her head and he shook his in response.

Her eyes again took in this unspeakable fiend who had crushed her body and her spirit beyond any possible resurgence. That one act on that sunny afternoon had robbed her of her youth—robbed her, until now, of any kind of normal relationship with a man. Had filled her, every second of every day and night, with terror that would stagger one's imagination. Had left her with a son… a son who, at least to all outward appearances, had taken on the morbid obsession to snuff the life out of helpless young girls. Like his father, his rage was starting to crack through. How far had it gone already? How much further would it go?

And to sit there showing no remorse whatsoever. He felt nothing for what she had been forced to live through. No feeling at all that he had infected her life in so many ways. If the glass and the guards and Jeff had not been there, would he jump her again? This question did not even need a response for the answer was right there in his eyes. He would do it again in a heartbeat… but this time, he would finish what he had meant to do eighteen years ago. And he would take perverse pleasure in the act… savoring every millisecond.

"Well, I can't say it's been a pleasure meeting you, but thank you for talking to me. I know you didn't have to. You have a right to say no. This visit answered a good many questions for me."

He nodded at her, then got up from his chair, but just as he was about to hang the phone up, he put it back to his ear. "It got me outta my cell for a while. But, I'll tell you; if your son's turned out like me, you better git some real good help for 'im or he might just go down the same road as his ol' man. It ain't no way to live your life."

"Is there anything I can get for you?" was the only thing she could think of to say.

"A pack o' cigarettes," he stated flatly.

"What brand?" she asked.

"Pall Malls."

"That's the same kind my son smokes," she said, aghast.

They watched him shuffle back out, then the iron door was slammed shut, echoing through the vast room.

"Well, this whole visit explains a lot," she said on their way out.

"What a scary son of a bitch!"

They went to the commissary where Shawna purchased a whole carton of cigarettes to be sent to Ivan Adler's cell. When they walked out to the parking lot, Jeff stopped and raised her chin to look into her eyes. "No regrets?"

"No regrets," she replied. "I don't think I could've gone on with my life not knowing what Jared's father was like… now I know. He's a killing machine." When they got into the car, she started shaking her head back and forth as if she could not stop. "He's not one bit sorry for how he hurt me. He has no feeling… no heart. Why did he do it?"

"Honey, no one knows why some men get off on killing. It makes no sense at all to normal people. All I can tell you is that he doesn't have the capacity to feel anything for the other person. He's completely self-absorbed. The world revolves around what he wants and to hell with everybody else. They're there for him to use as he pleases."

"I didn't really expect him to be sorry. A man who would rape and murder so many people couldn't possibly have any guilt or shame. In a way, it's easier to deal with a complete monster than if he were a real human being who had been severely abused as a child and was appalled at what he'd done. He had no compunction about what he did to me, but he didn't give a rat's ass about any of his victims. It's sort of like being attacked by a wild animal."

"He's got a lot of mental problems, Shawna, on top of chemical imbalances in his brain. He has such an undeveloped personality—a true psychopath."

"He's a soulless murderer—no doubt about that. Jeff, do you think I should tell Jared the truth about me being his real mother… and about his real father?"

"Oh, I don't know, honey. That's a pretty heavy thing to lay on anyone—especially someone with problems as deep as Jared's. It might be intensely disturbing to him. I mean, he thinks he's had a wonderful, stable family. News like this could really push him over the edge."

"I just thought he had a right to know about his real heritage. Maybe when he's a lot older. But only if he really straightens out. He for sure couldn't handle it the way he is now."

They ate dinner at a Japanese restaurant in downtown Salem and spent the night at the only upscale hotel in town. They spent the weekend exploring feelings—anger, sorrow, pity, sadness, relief, and emotional and spiritual growth. They both shared their deepest fears, allowing all defense walls to melt away—each bearing their soul to the other. They spoke through tears and laughter. Communicated dreams and hopes for the future. It was the most healing time of Shawna's life. An unspoken feeling of deep soul bonding filled both of them to overflowing.

CHAPTER 28

On the next Tuesday morning, Jeff received a call from Shawna telling him that the house had sold and she was going to have to fly back to Oregon the next weekend to sign the papers and close the deal. "Life is so crazy," she said. "Why couldn't this have happened last weekend when we were up there anyway?"

"Do you want me to go with you?" he asked.

"Oh no, I'll go by myself, honey. Thank you for offering though."

"What about Jared? He'll have his wheels back by then, won't he?"

"Yeah, that's right. He's been bugging me non stop to take it to my mechanic."

"Just tell him that I'll look at it for him. Tell him I'm real clever with engines. Then I'll replace the part Kev and I pilfered."

"Good idea. But what about this weekend? He might… you know."

"How about if Kevin and I follow him in Kevin's car. He's never seen it. We'll be sure to eat and pee before we go."

Shawna chuckled. "Would you do that? Oh, then I won't be worried sick that he's gonna do something."

"You know I'll do it, sweetheart. I wouldn't sleep anyway, thinking he's running around loose out there."

Kevin was more than willing, even excited, to go out on a stakeout with his buddy. Jeff had apprised him of the whole saga about Shawna's childhood attack and resulting pregnancy. Kevin's jaw dropped almost to the floor at this unspeakable atrocity. He told Jeff that he had long suspected that there was something she was hiding, but he certainly did not expect it to be anything close to this horror story.

He picked Jeff up from his house at two o'clock in the afternoon, then they went to have lunch before taking their place on Shawna's street. They picked a spot where they could keep Jared's car in plain view. They were both wearing baseball caps and Kevin had brought a fake beard and mustache for Jeff to wear. "I wore this as part of my Halloween costume last year… remember?"

They both laughed hysterically when he put it on, but Jeff thought it was a great idea. He thought he could fool even his own mother in this disguise. He had instructed Kevin not to drink too much liquid, but he brought a portable facility just in case—a coffee can with a plastic snap-on lid.

They sat for several hours, then Jared appeared in the carport with something wrapped in a dark-colored blanket—something long like a baseball bat. He put the article in the trunk of his car, then got in holding a piece of paper in his hand. He pulled out onto the street. They hung back at a safe distance and followed him. He got on the freeway for a good twenty miles, then exited.

To their surprise, he pulled over to the side of the road as soon as he made a right turn on the first street. "Oh shit! He's stopping!" Kevin could not stop in time, so he drove past him and pulled into a private driveway where they kept an eagle eye on him. Their lights were turned off and they sat watching him, hoping to God that he did not catch sight of them. They were a few houses down, but right, smack in front of him.

Jared's dome light went on. "It looks like he's reading a piece of paper. Probably a map," Kevin observed.

"He must be going somewhere unknown to him. This is getting really weird… I just hope…"

"The perp's on the move," Kevin interrupted. "He's driving right past us. He didn't look over. I'm sure he didn't see us."

"The 'perp'?" Jeff asked.

"Uh huh. Perpetrator, I heard it on TV."

"Oh."

Kevin slowly backed the car out of the driveway and followed Jared for several blocks before turning his lights back on. They tailed him for about five miles making several turns. Finally, Jared pulled in to the parking lot of a large, neighborhood park. It was dark and deserted. Kevin again shut off his headlights. They watched from a good distance, as Jared pulled into a space in the far corner of the lot. He sat in his car for a while, then the door swung open and he stepped out. He opened his trunk and took the blanket and whatever was inside out and tucked it under his arm. He started walking down a dirt pathway into the park.

"Where the hell is he going?" Jeff said.

"I don't know, but we better follow him, huh?"

Jeff looked over at his friend, "This is fucking scary!"

"I think I just aged twenty years in the last twenty seconds!"

Kevin pulled his car up onto the grass, under a low hanging tree where Jared would not spot it when he came back to the parking lot. They got out and slowly made their way into the park where Jared had entered seconds ago. They walked softly and tried to stay within the concealment of bushes as much as they could. All of a sudden, Kevin burst into violent gyrations—turning, twisting, arms flailing wildly. "What the hell are you doing?" Jeff barked in a hushed voice.

"I just walked through a friggin' spider web!" he exclaimed as he continued his hysterical brushing frenzy—wiping madly at the disgusting feeling mesh that was stuck to his face, hair and clothing.

"Jesus Christ!" Jeff could not stifle his gut laugh. "Get a grip… the whole world's going to know we're here."

"If I just walked through the cobweb, where the hell is the cob?" Kevin demanded, still brushing. Jeff just shook his head. Funny thing, that spider web dance.

They walked past a small duck pond, then they spotted Jared sitting at a picnic table next to a restroom. Kevin extended his arm in front of Jeff to stop him from taking another step. He gestured for him to retreat into a cluster of bushes far enough to remain unnoticed, but close enough to keep Jared in clear view.

"He's keeps looking around like he's expecting company," Kevin whispered. Jeff nodded. They stayed crouched in their hiding place for at least an hour, their senses on full alert. Their frazzled nerves along with the icy chill of the night air were causing both of them to shiver uncontrollably.

Jared got up and started pacing around as if becoming impatient. At one point, he unzipped his pants and took out his penis. They watched him step over to a garbage can and urinate. He stood over the trash receptacle for a long time with his back to them. "I don't even wanna know what he's doing," Jeff whispered. "Perverted fuck."

Finally, he zipped up and grabbed the object from the picnic table and started back towards the parking lot. He walked right past them without any notice. They were well camouflaged; however, they could have been discovered if Jared had been a little more aware of his surroundings. They waited for a few minutes before emerging from their hideout.

"Looks like his Saturday night date didn't show," Kevin said.

"Whomever it was has no idea how lucky she is. This one's gonna live to eat tomorrow's breakfast."

Once more, they made their way back to the parking lot ducking behind cover as much as possible. They stopped at the edge of the park where they were well concealed behind a wooden fence that led to a playground for little kids. They observed Jared putting the object back into his trunk. He got into his car and pulled out, making a right turn onto the street.

By the time they made it back to Kevin's car and started in the direction Jared had gone, they had lost sight of him. They drove around the perimeter of the park and up and down side streets, but no sign of the silver Accord.

"Shit, we lost him," Kevin barked. "What should we do?"

"Let's go back to the apartment to see if he goes straight home. I hope to shit he does!"

When they got back to the apartment, Kevin drove through the alley to check for Jared's car. There it was in space number eleven. "Oh, thank God," Jeff moaned.

They parked and waited for a while to make sure Jared was not going out again. Convinced that he was in for the night, they took off for home. Shawna would be back Sunday afternoon so their work was done until next weekend. They both heaved a big sigh of relief having no idea what was taking place at that very moment upstairs in Shawna's den.

CHAPTER 29

Jared had pulled up a chair at his computer—logged on to the net. "I was there. Where were you?" he typed in.

"I couldn't get out. I'm sorry. My dumb parents are watching me like a hawk with this serial killer loose."

"I know just what you mean," he lied. "My parents are really lame too. Maybe another time, huh?"

"Fuck my stupid parents. I want to meet you so bad. I sense that you're really cute! I can sneak out my bedroom window after they go to bed. Are you up for it?"

"Yeah, sure. What time?" he typed in.

"Ten o'clock. They'll be sawin' logs by then."

"Same place?"

"Same place."

Shawna arrived home at two in the afternoon the next day. She had signed all of the papers and the house in which she had grown up now belonged to someone else—a young couple expecting their first baby. She had ambivalent feelings about letting it go. It was the last link to her life with her beloved mother and father. It was the only place they had ever lived as a family. But it also held some of the worst memories of her life. Memories she was eager to deal with in therapy so that she could really put them behind her this time. With the love she and Jeff now shared, she was filled with optimism about the future for the first time since her attack.

Jared's car was in the carport so she figured he was in his room. She knocked on his door and received no answer. She knocked louder, then opened the door a crack. He was sound asleep in his bed. How could he still be asleep at two o'clock in the afternoon? she thought. What a lazy bum. She closed the door deciding to let him sleep. She was secretly glad not to have to deal with him right now anyway. She went into her room to call Jeff.

They traded stories of their weekend adventures. Her telling him that the house was all wrapped up. Him telling her in detail exactly what he and Kevin had observed on Saturday night. They hung up after making plans to get together the next weekend. Shawna would drive to his house and spend Friday night, and then they would resume their Saturday night surveillance.

The Tuesday evening news reported a new victim. It was a young teenage girl whose body was found dumped into the Los Angeles River. Poor thing was viciously raped and beaten to death. When Jeff saw the news clip, he immediately called Shawna. "Honey, it's not Jared! We know he didn't have contact with anyone that night. We made sure he went home after we followed him to that park."

"I know! I just saw the report. Oh, thank God it's not Jared! I'm so, so relieved."

"Me too, whew!" He released a big sigh. "I guess that detective was right that all kinds of people are thinking it's someone they know. But we sure had reason to suspect Jared."

"Didn't we though? Now that we know it's not him, I'm gonna focus on getting him some major help. The best—before something awful does happen."

"Absolutely. Maybe UCLA. They're up on all this stuff. But

honey, now we know he's not the Saturday Night Killer then what was he doing in that park the other night?"

"Yeah, that's true. What was he doing there?" she puzzled. "Maybe he was gonna make contact with some other sicko to buy more of that porno stuff."

"I bet that's exactly what he was doing. Still, I wonder what was inside the blanket."

"Maybe nothing. You said it was freezing that night."

"No, there was something in there. Something long and solid."

"Could it have been something he was gonna trade for the magazines or films?"

"Maybe."

It took several weeks to get an appointment, but Shawna arranged for a day off from work mid-week so that she could take Jared for tests and an evaluation.

The doctors could not have had a less eager patient on their hands. He started answering questions in his typical, monotone—one or two word responses—but the expertise of these medical professionals gradually got him to open up about his thoughts and fantasies. They also interviewed Shawna at length, then did a battery of medical tests on Jared. It took all day.

She and Jared returned the next week for the results and to discuss what action to take. First, the doctor called Shawna into his office for a private talk. "I'm not going to sugar coat it—your son's in trouble," he stated point blank. "We do agree with earlier findings that he does indeed have Antisocial and Schizoid Disorder, but his problems go way beyond that. His psychological workup has us very concerned. This boy has aberrant, sadistic sexual fantasies that we believe he is likely to act out in a violent manner. He has all the signs of being a sociopath—no interest or feeling for anyone outside of himself. He appears to have no conscience and no regard for life. He could be a ticking time bomb about to go off."

"It's that bad?" she asked, her eyes sharply focused on the doctor's distraught expression.

"He needs to be watched carefully. Have you observed anything other than the pornography and the rope for auto-erotic practices?"

"One thing I forgot to tell you last week—just before my mother went into the hospital, she caught him peeping into a neighbor girl's window. He told her it was the first time and it wouldn't happen again."

"It's more than likely that it was not the first time and not the last," the doctor informed. "I'm going to prescribe some medications for him. Be sure he takes them. Also, I want him into long-term therapy immediately. I have a doctor I can refer who's close to where you live." He sat across from her at his desk writing out several prescriptions. He handed them to her with a look of grave seriousness on his face. He then asked her to send Jared in and wait for him in the reception area.

Jared came out to rejoin his sister in the waiting room about twenty minutes later with a malevolent look on his face. He talked little on their way home. Shawna stopped to fill the prescriptions at a drugstore near the apartment.

Right away, she dispensed the indicated dosage of each medication to him. The doctor had scared her into a frenzy with the urgency of his demeanor. Jared tried to resist, but she wasn't backing down this time. She even made him open his mouth for inspection after he swallowed the pills. A disgusting thing—looking into his mouth. She thought to herself that if he started giving her crap about taking them in the future, she would slip them into his food somehow.

CHAPTER 30

"God Jeff, that doctor scared the bejesus outta me. He was so adamant about getting Jared on meds and into therapy right away," she said as she sat across from him at Pedro's.

"Really? Well, even though he's not the Saturday Night Killer, we know he's a tad disturbed."

"But they seemed to think he could be violent in acting out his sexual fantasies."

"I sure hope we got him before he hurt anyone."

She nodded as she let out a big sigh. "But I have to stand over him to make him take his meds. If I didn't force him, he'd never bother with it. I can't baby sit him for the rest of his life. Now here we go on that subject again. What am I gonna do with him?"

"Well, maybe once the medications start to take effect, he'll be easier to reason with."

"You think?"

"Maybe he'll start to want normal relationships with girls instead of these perverted fantasies."

"Oh, I hope so."

As the weeks went by, Jared did seem to come out of his isolation a bit. He was somewhat more conversational and Shawna no longer needed to nag him constantly about his hygiene. To her shock, he even got a job all on his own volition. He was hired by a super market to do general maintenance. His duties consisted of keeping the parking lot clean and collecting all of the baskets and bringing them back to the front of the store. He was also the one they summoned when something was spilled or broken. It only paid minimum wage, but he seemed perfectly content with this job. He did not need to interact with other people very much and the work was easy. It also gave him his own money, which pleased him immensely. He no longer had to beg his sister for gas money or spending cash—a process that was beginning to get on his nerves. The only thing that did bother Shawna was that he was gone from the apartment more than before. But things seemed to be progressing so she decided not to press him about his comings and goings.

The Saturday Night Killer had not been caught, but police kept saying that they were close to making an arrest. The murders had slowed down to about one every four weeks. Perhaps that was due to the inclement weather they were experiencing in Southern California that winter. It was extremely cold and windy with heavy rainstorms blowing in from the North. Shawna kept up with the news reports, but was resting so much easier now that she knew it had nothing to do with her son.

Jared still had his job at the supermarket, although his enthusiasm for the work took a nosedive since he was forced to carry out his duties in the freezing cold and torrential rains. He had an aversion to getting wet. Shawna always blamed this personality quirk for his lack of interest in bathing or showering.

One disturbing thing that had caught Shawna's attention was that Jared seemed to be gradually misplacing every piece of clothing that she had bought him. When she would question him, she would inevitably receive a detached "I don't know" shrug. As quickly as she replaced his lost shirts and pants, they would go missing again. Finally, in a rage, she shouted to him, "You can just go naked for all I care! I'm done giving in to this disappearing act your clothes seem to be doing. You've got money. Go buy your own clothes. If you have to spend your own paycheck, maybe you'll keep better track of them."

Although separating herself from Jared's company was ever present on Shawna's mind, she was flabbergasted on the morning he announced that he had found a small apartment in North Hollywood and would be moving out at the end of the month. He had already given the landlord a deposit.

"Well, how much is the rent?" she inquired.

"Five hundred a month."

"I don't see how you found any apartment for that price. And even so, you only bring home eight hundred a month. You won't have anything left for food, utilities, insurance, clothes and gas. What if your car needs repairs? Oh Jared, you're going off half-baked with this plan. You can't begin to afford your own place yet."

"I can do it! I'm eighteen now. I do what I want."

"Honey, I'm not trying to burst your bubble. It's just that you have no idea how expensive it is to support your own household. If you could just wait for a little longer..."

"Then I'll get another job," he interrupted. "I'm movin' out the first of the month."

"I guess it's pointless to argue with you. But I want you to come back if you can't make it by yourself, okay?"

"I'll be okay. I can make it."

"And you have to keep up with your therapy and your meds. Do you swear?"

"Whatever."

"No whatever. Do you swear? You know Mom's looking down from heaven all the time so don't lie to me."

Jared appeared shaken as he gave her an odd look—then responded with, "I said I will!"

"Hello beautiful," Jeff's voice resonated over the phone.

"Hi handsome," Shawna responded. "You'll never guess what?"

"No more wild surprises. I can't take it!"

She laughed. "Just one more. Jared's moving out on the first."

"What?"

"He just announced it to me. Said he put down a deposit on a five hundred dollar a month apartment in North Hollywood."

"No kidding? Well, maybe he'll learn some responsibility. See what's really involved in supporting himself."

"Still, I don't see how he can make ends meet on his piddly income. But hey, what do I know? He seems to have it all figured out."

"He'll be beggin' for a loan within the first month," Jeff laughed.

"I know."

"Have you seen the place yet?"

"No. I'm going over there with him on Saturday. Wanna come?"

"Sure. I'll treat you both to a nice lunch," he offered. "Sound okay?"

"Sounds wonderful. I miss you."

"Me too—BIG time! Pick you up at eleven?"

"Great."

Jeff was meeting Kevin at Pedro's after work that evening. They had been keeping their usual Wednesday dinner date. There was always so much to discuss about the goings on in both of their lives.

"Over here," Jeff shouted as he waved at Kevin who was just walking past the hostess's desk. He was always the first to arrive so he got them a table and ordered their drinks. Kevin appreciated sitting right down to a nice margarita after a hard day of work.

"Have a tough day?" Jeff inquired.

"A full day. So much driving in God-awful traffic. I'm really ready for a good drink and a killer dinner."

"This is the place. How's May?" Jeff asked.

"April, you putz!"

"Okay April. How's it going?"

"Turns out she has two little kids. I'm not a fanatic like you, but I'd like to start my own family when I get married. From scratch. No these are mine, those are yours—let's have some more that are ours."

"So she's out of the picture?"

"She's out, but Cassie's in. I met this dynamite girl at work. I had lunch in the cafeteria, which I rarely do considering the slop they serve. But I'm really glad I did. I was eating at a table by myself and she sat down at the table next to me. She was a stone fox. I kid you not. Well, I asked what department she worked in and we started up a whole conversation that led to a date Saturday night. We had an awesome time. I think she might be the one!"

"'The one?' After one date? And you tell me I rush in too fast. Does she have kids?"

"No way. She lives with a roommate. Never been married. No rug rats. I want you to meet this one."

"That serious, huh? Not this weekend, but the one after I think we could get together. How about if Shawna and I cook dinner at my house."

"Cool. Let's set it up."

Jeff said he would consult with Shawna and if it were okay with her, all systems would be go. He then filled Kevin in on all of the latest on Jared—that he was moving into his own place in North Hollywood. Kevin agreed that this was a good thing. He needed to experience the real world out on his own. The conversation again drifted back to Kevin's new heartthrob, Cassie, and stayed there throughout dinner.

CHAPTER 31

As they drove up to the address, they saw a freestanding bungalow with an attached, makeshift carport. There were three other identical units generously spaced out on the oversized piece of property.

The landscaping consisted of dirt, several dead trees and the entire property overgrown with weeds. Each unit was marred with graffiti on old, decaying wood siding. There were cavernous holes in the rotting wood and the roofs were all patched and repatched with patches on top of those.

"People actually live here?" Jeff blurted.

"Yeah, I got the only vacancy," Jared said.

"You lucky thing."

Shawna was still standing at the curb in stunned silence. When a clear thought finally took shape in her head, all she could say was, "Oh, my God!"

"What?" Jared hissed. "It's just till I git some money saved. Then I'll move."

"Well…, you said the landlord gave you the key already. Let's see what the inside looks like," Shawna said with morbid trepidation.

All three stepped up on the tiny wooden porch while Jared pulled open what once was a screen door and with some difficulty, waggled the key into the corroded door lock. He tried repeatedly to get the key to turn, but it was rusted solid.

"Here, let me try," said Jeff. He switched places with Jared and began to work the lock. After a few minutes of struggle, the key not budging, he leaned against the door and it flew open. He found himself standing in the middle of the living room. Shawna just looked at Jared with an "okay, you can tell me this is a joke now" expression.

Jeff turned to them and made his signature sweeping arm motion. "Don't just stand there, come on in."

Jeff and Shawna looked around with eyes wide and jaws dropped. They were standing on a wooden floor. Not hardwood floors—just a wood floor. Wood that seemed anxious to inject a multitude of slivers into exposed flesh if one were to walk about barefoot. The walls were also wood—just the same as the floor. Not painted. Nothing was—inside or out. They saw hundreds of cockroaches scampering into gaping crevices and cobwebs that created a thick covering in the corners and all along the baseboards. Immediately underneath the windowsill sat a humungous black widow spider. Jeff walked over and stomped the spider with the sole of his shoe.

There was an old couch that was so filthy; one could barely discern that it was once gold and black velvet. A scarred up wooden end table sat to the right of it hosting a metal lamp with a pull chain—no shade, just a dust-covered bulb.

"Shall we continue our tour into the bedroom?" Jeff asked.

"This is it," Jared answered. "It's a studio apartment. Just one main room."

"Oh, I see—a studio apartment," Jeff said with a mocking raise of his eyebrow. Then he proceeded into what he thought must be the kitchen. Shawna stood in the doorway, too repulsed to make a complete entrance.

The kitchen sink stood alone with no countertops at all. It was badly stained white porcelain with the visible pipes wrapped in some kind of old, disintegrating tape. Jeff turned on the faucet then wiggled the loose sink back and forth from the wall. After several seconds, a brown colored liquid began drizzling out of the spigot. He quickly turned the squeaking handle back to the off position and the water gradually slowed to a drip. Against the opposite wall stood a grimy old stove with four burners and a waist high refrigerator that looked fairly new.

He looked up into Shawna's incredulous face. "I can't wait to see the bathroom." They all stepped to the opposite side of the living room and into a very small doorway, which Jeff had to enter sideways to fit through. There was a toilet with no lid (also loose from the floor), a sink and a square shower that stood in the corner taking up most of the room. The shower curtain was salmon and black and moldy and was coming undone from its hooks. That was all. No cupboard space, no medicine cabinet, no tub, no towel racks. A teeny window with bars on the outside sat high up on the wall above the sink. The whole place reeked of mold and God knew what else.

Jeff turned to address himself to Jared and Shawna, "I guess we've seen it all."

"Boy, I thought the house I grew up in was a dump. This takes "dump" to a whole new level. Did you even look at this place before you rented it?" she grilled Jared.

"Naturally I did."

"Are you insane? This hovel isn't even fit for the cockroaches."

"I don't need nothin' fancy."

"Fancy?! You can't live here. This is… it's… I'm speechless!" Her hands were covering her face in shock. "You surely didn't commit to this. You couldn't pay me five million dollars a month to live in this rat hole. It's…it's disgusting—depressing. And it's making me sick. I'm sick to my stomach."

"It's only for a while, Shawna. I said I'd git a better place as soon as I can." His patience was beginning to wear thin and she could sense a full-blown battle coming.

"Does it even have heat?" she asked.

"Yeah, there's a furnace in the wall between the living room and the kitchen."

First Shawna flushed the toilet to see if it was functional, then she went to turn on the furnace to check it out. It kicked on; however, the most pungent odor started pouring into the room—so strong that it overpowered the rest of the repugnant smells that permeated the place.

"It probably hasn't been on in a while," Jared defended. "The rent's cheap 'cause the place needs some work."

"What it really needs is the demolition ball," Jeff offered.

Shawna shut the furnace off quickly then she turned and looked Jared straight in the eye. He looked down. "You're not living in a shithole like this. You'd be better off pitching a tent!"

With eyes cast down, he spoke in a voice that clearly indicated that his mind was made up. "You can't stop me. You're not my mother!"

She and Jeff locked eyes and he read her thoughts. He subtly shook his head "no". "You're right Jared, I'm not your mother. If you really want to live this way, it's your decision. You're eighteen now—old enough to make your own mistakes. I'm gonna say one more thing, then I'll stop lecturing. You must keep yourself and your clothes clean. There's no laundry room so you'll have to go out to a Laundromat or bring your stuff to my place. I'm telling you right now, Jared, if you become dirty and smelly again, you'll get fired from your job. No one in the world is gonna hire someone who stinks. The minute your hygiene goes, you'll find yourself unemployed. Do you get that?"

"Yeah," he answered defensively.

"When are you planning to move in?"

"Now. He said I could move in early—no extra charge."

"How generous."

The next day, Shawna went out and bought a ton of things Jared needed so that he wouldn't be living in total squalor. Jeff helped clean and fix the things that were loose and broken. He hung a new shower curtain and mounted a medicine cabinet with a nice large mirror over the sink in the bathroom. They hung some colorful curtains over the bare windows and they bought him a microwave oven with a stand and a small table with two chairs for the kitchen. They bought pillows; sheets, blankets, an alarm clock and Shawna broke down and bought him more new clothes. Then they helped him move all of his belongings in. Both Jeff and Shawna kept their eyes peeled for more magazines and videos (or anything else incriminating), but did not spot anything amiss this time. If he still had these things, he must have been hiding them somewhere—perhaps in the trunk of his car.

"This is just till we can get you into a better place—and give me your number as soon as your phone is installed okay?" Shawna said.

"Okay." Jared was in a big hurry. He could barely survive a day without his Internet access.

The next Friday evening, Shawna accompanied Jeff to an awards dinner that his company was giving in order to acknowledge the accomplishments of its most valued employees. Jeff was to receive one of the highest awards, as his most recent project, the baby doll, was his most successful contribution to the company to date. It quickly became the toy to have for little girls between five and fifteen. They carried the doll around in soft blankets, car seats and strollers. An entire ensemble of bottles, diapers, blankets and colorful clothing were abundantly available to go with baby. Jeff had named her, "Baby Brittany," one of the most popular names of the day. Stores could not keep them in stock. They were bought up as soon as they hit the shelves and the company owed this runaway hit to the man who created it in his own imagination.

Shawna drove over to Jeff's house as they had planned to spend the entire weekend together just resting, watching movies they had rented, taking Duffy for walks and cooking meals together. The company dinner and the remainder of the weekend were eagerly anticipated by both of them. They needed a few days to veg out. A time with no appointments—no obligations.

Jeff answered the door all dressed in his black tux. He swooned when he laid eyes on his date. Shawna was wearing an emerald green evening dress—low cut and form fitting satin on top, then gathered at the waist with layers of shear silk cascading over a loose fitting satin skirt that flowed into a leg flattering scalloped hemline. Around her neck was a white gold and diamond necklace that fell enticingly between her breasts and dangling from her lovely ears were the diamond drop earrings Jeff had given her for Christmas. Her long chestnut hair fell loosely down her back and she had a green, cashmere shawl thrown over her shoulders. "You look gorgeous!" they said to each other in unison. Laughing, they embraced.

"I have the most beautiful date at the function," Jeff told her.

"How do you know? You haven't seen the other women yet."

"I don't need to," he stated with conviction. "No one can hold a candle to my Shawna."

She looked deeply into his eyes and smiled with affection. She thought that no other woman's happiness could equal hers. She had waited for thirty-one years and had certainly found the most wonderful man alive.

"I can't wait to watch my love receive his accolade tonight. I'm so proud of you, darling."

"Thank you, baby. It wouldn't mean half as much if you weren't here to share it with me."

The function was held in a large banquet room at the Century Plaza Hotel in Century City. The turnout was at least three hundred people from all different departments within the company and their spouses.

After cocktails and dinner were enjoyed, the corporate CEO stepped up onto the podium to announce the names of the award winners. Each person received applause as he or she walked up to accept a plaque and a bonus check.

The MC went into a long narrative, gushing praises and heartfelt gratitude as he announced the last name of the evening, "Jeffrey Scott Daniels for his creation of 'Baby Brittany!'" The entire room stood to give an embarrassingly long (and loud) ovation.

Jeff walked up and was presented with a gold engraved plaque and an envelope containing his bonus check. "Well, I always thought that I was robbed of my childhood having to take care of eleven little brothers and sisters, but now I see the method to God's madness. For survival purposes, I had to know what would capture and hold kids' attention so that I could steel a moment's reprieve for myself. Each pittance of time felt like a stay of execution."

The crowd roared, then Jeff continued, "When I ran out of manufactured toys that would keep the kids occupied, I was forced to get busy with my own creations. I was beyond thrilled that my makeshift contraptions held their attention even better than most of the store bought toys. This is when I knew what my future would be." He said a heartfelt "thank you" to everyone for all of their assistance and support as he blew a kiss out to the audience.

Shawna was beaming for this was a side of Jeff about which she knew little—his professional side. When he sat back down next to her, he leaned over and whispered in her ear, "God, I love you."

CHAPTER 32

When they awoke the next morning, the three of them were snuggled together in the middle of the cozy king-sized bed. "What time is it?" Shawna asked.

Jeff turned and glanced at the digital clock on the nightstand. "Ten-thirty," he responded. Duffy lifted his head, licked Jeff's cheek, then lay back down between them to catch a few more zs.

"I almost feel guilty basking here in paradise while Jared's existing in that broken down shack. Is it all right if I try his number? I haven't been able to get him on the phone all week. It's either a busy signal or no answer."

"All teenagers are on line most of the time. I can't for the life of me figure out what they talk about in those stupid chat rooms for hours on end," he said as he passed her the telephone.

She dialed and again received a busy signal. "I'll try again in a little while," she said. But an hour later there was no answer. "Jeff, I'm a little worried. Not that anything's gonna happen to him, but that he might be getting into something. It's a nagging feeling in the pit of my stomach. I just don't trust him after everything we found."

"Would you like to take a drive over there this afternoon? We can just pop in to check on him. Make sure he's okay. We could take Duffy, but I'm afraid he'll get splinters in his paws."

"Oh, you're so sweet to take me. I just don't wanna ruin your day by going over there. We can just see how he's doing—

ask if he needs anything, then how about if we come back and take Duffy for a hike in the mountains?"

"Sounds good," he said, throwing on his robe. "I'll whip us up some breakfast."

Jeff decided to take Duffy along to Jared's place. They would only be there for a few minutes, then they could drive to a spectacular trail he knew of in the hills above the valley.

"He wouldn't do anything to hurt an animal, would he?"

"Funny you ask that, but no, he doesn't even notice animals. When he was a little boy, we would take him to the zoo, but he had no interest at all. We would all be enjoying watching each animal and reading about them and he would just be looking off in some other direction, worlds away—inside his little idiot head. He never paid any attention to the family pets we had either."

"You definitely have resentment towards him, don't you?"

She covered her face with her hands, then, "God, Jeff, I do. I've resented that little shit from day one. He was never like any little boy I've ever known. First, I hated him because I was forced to give birth to that maniac's baby. Then, he started showing signs of being the same type of creature. He was always so unlovable— so off into himself. So damn cold and unresponsive. I hate myself for saying these things—for even thinking them. Mom would say, 'we should never think such thoughts.'"

Jeff grabbed her hand. "You certainly should think such thoughts!" he exclaimed. "He is different. It's very hard to feel any warmth towards him when he feels nothing for anyone else."

She gave him a look of such gratitude; he felt shivers running up and down his spine.

"You know, as I think back, mom and dad seemed to have a hard time loving him too. They would never admit it, but it was almost as if they had to force themselves to show love towards him too. When he was a baby, they adored him. I don't know.

The love I felt from them was incredible, but after Jared started growing up, he was such a thorn to our family—never responding to any affection or attention at all..."

"Honey, you don't have to apologize for the way you feel. I wouldn't love him either—even if he were born from my loins. Just because you gave birth to someone doesn't mean that they are anything like you. They may be a lost soul—like Jared seems to be."

"We all tried with every ounce of our being to help him to fit in—to teach him how to love, but it all falls on deaf ears. He has no interest in becoming a decent person."

"We can't help some people, honey," Jeff told her. "Some people are beyond help."

"He's beyond help."

They parked at the curb in front of Jared's humble abode and Jeff put Duffy's leash on. They stepped up onto the little porch and Shawna knocked. No answer. She knocked again. Still nothing. No sound at all coming from inside. She walked around to the carport and saw that his car was gone.

"Well, he's not home. What should we do?"

"Why don't we go in and look around?"

"How are we gonna get in?"

Jeff leaned his weight against the door and it opened easily. "Somehow I knew he wouldn't have gotten this fixed."

They peeked in and called for him and when they knew the coast was clear, they went inside and closed the front door. Jeff took Duffy's leash off and turned to Shawna. "This place smells even worse than it did the first time. Are you up for another look around?"

"Ah huh. Let's see what he has this time—now that he thinks no one will ever come in here."

The place was extremely messy, as they had anticipated.

"There's his TV right where we put it when we moved him in. Looks like it hasn't even been plugged in," Shawna said, pointing to the corner. They looked through drawers and closets, under cushions and beneath the bed. They found an abundance of incriminating materials. More smut magazines—different from the ones they had discovered before. These were even worse. More videos of the same nature. They saw the rope with the noose. This time it was tied to a hook Jared had pounded into the wall beside the sofa. There was a blown up picture of a woman's crotch taped to the wall just above his computer—at perfect eye level while he was busy in his "chat rooms."

"Is there any sense in booting up the computer? It'll probably be the same porno sites as before."

"Don't bother. He's no better at all," she sighed. "He wanted his own place so that he could bury himself completely in his porno world. I thought the medications might have been helping, but they're not. He's sick beyond medication. He needs a new brain."

Just then something snagged Jeff's attention. He picked up a piece of paper with some writing on it, 405 to 5 to 8 east. S.D. 619- the rest of the number had been torn off. He handed the paper to Shawna. "Looks like the area code and directions to San Diego, doesn't it?"

She studied the writing. "Yeah. What else could it be? But if he's driving down there, why didn't he take the directions?"

"Maybe he got a more detailed map off the Internet or from a person."

"Maybe that's where he is today."

"Maybe."

They gave each other a somber look of dread. Why would Jared be driving to San Diego? He didn't know anyone down there. He had no friends. It appeared that he was getting all of the smut that he wanted right here. So what the hell was he doing?

"Oh Jeff, what should we do?"

"There's nothing we can do. Let's just wait and see. A guy certainly isn't breaking any laws by taking a drive to another city. I mean, the police would really think we were wacked if we called them in a panic because Jared drove to San Diego."

They left everything where they had found it and made their exit. In the car, Jeff diligently inspected Duffy's paws for splinters, then looked up at Shawna. "I know we're both worried, but let's try to enjoy the rest of the weekend. We'll look into this next week. Our hands are tied for the moment."

"You know, my mother's estate should be coming through in a few more months. She had left instructions with me to dole Jared's half out to him in installments—five thousand dollars a year. Said she was afraid he'd blow the whole thing in six months if he got the twenty-five thousand in one lump sum."

Jeff nodded. "I agree with your mom. This way, he'll have a new nest egg every year till the estate runs out. That'll get him through the next five years anyway. By then, maybe he'll have gotten himself into a more lucrative job situation."

"I sure hope so. But, for the time being, it'll get him into a decent apartment."

CHAPTER 34

The next Saturday night, Jeff and Shawna cooked dinner for Kevin and Cassie. They loved Cassie right away. She was cute and funny—a good match for Kevin, they thought. Shawna recognized her from work. She had recalled passing her in the halls on occasion. They talked shop for a while, then played a game where they all shared stories of their most embarrassing moments—a suggestion of Cassie's. It turned out to be a sidesplitting evening. When they said goodnight, they promised to get together again soon. As the couple walked out, Kevin leaned his head back in, "Well? Isn't she great?"

"She's dynamite, Kev. You really did hit the jackpot this time," Jeff affirmed with a thumbs up gesture.

Kevin beamed under the praise of his new honey. "See ya at Pedro's Wednesday."

Jeff and Shawna cleaned up the dinner dishes and went to bed. When they were all cuddled up, Jeff clicked on the TV. They watched a detective show, then the eleven o'clock news came on. They were both riveted to the television to see if there was anything about the Saturday Night Killer. Sure enough, the fourth story was about the body of a junior high school girl found raped, beaten to death and left in a city park in San Diego. The murder was believed to have taken place sometime last Saturday night.

They glared into each other's eyes in paralyzed shock. "In San Diego! In a city park!" Jeff shouted.

"Oh God!" Shawna screamed.

"This is damn serious. Before, in the back of my mind, I thought it just couldn't be him. Now I know it's him!" he exclaimed. "I'm calling the police right now!"

He immediately picked up the telephone and dialed 911. "I'm sorry sir, this number is for reporting emergencies."

"You wouldn't call a girl getting murdered an emergency?"

"You'll have to hang up and call your local police station. They'll take your information." She hung up.

Jeff called directory assistance and got the number for the police department. After telling his story, he was switched to different people five times. Finally, he got a detective that covered the North Hollywood area on the line. Relieved to be turning this ugly assignment over to authorities, he laid out all of the facts to the officer—everything they had found in the past few months along with Jared's suspicious comings and goings.

"Your name?"

"Jeffrey Daniels."

"Your address?"

Jeff gave it, becoming noticeably irritated. At last, the detective asked for Jared's address.

"We'll send an officer out to question him. I can't guarantee just when he'll be able to get there, but I'll try to put a rush on it."

"You've got to act quickly. Before anyone else loses their life. And you won't tell him who reported him, will you?"

"Absolutely not. Your name will not be given. Not to worry about that."

Jeff hung the phone up and turned to Shawna, "They're gonna send someone out to question him."

"When?" she asked.

"I don't know. He said as soon as possible—whatever that means. I guess we just have to wait."

"I'm petrified, Jeff."

"Me too, honey. Me too."

They were on pins and needles for the next two weeks, the news reporting yet another murder of an eighteen year old. This time the killer had snuck right into her apartment, which she shared with another girl. The roommate was out on a date at the time. The body was found bludgeoned and strangled (no obvious signs of sexual assault) and lying faced down on the bedroom floor. "But this time," the news reporter went on, "there was a real good eyewitness. Apparently, the young girl had ordered a pizza and the deliveryman was just walking up when he saw the perpetrator tear past him with blood spatter all over his clothing. He had gotten a good look at the man and ran out to see what vehicle he took off in. He got the plate number."

Finally, Jeff received a call at work. "Jeffrey Daniels?" a male voice inquired.

"Yes."

"This is detective Bernard. I just wanted to tell you that we did go out there and interview Jared Reese at his home. After a lengthy interrogation, we don't feel that he has any connection with these crimes. He doesn't fit the profile. We're looking for a much older man. In fact, we're very close to making an arrest."

"Wait a minute. I'm sure it's him."

"I agree he's a little peculiar… okay, a lot peculiar, but we don't feel he's our man and we have nothing to connect him with any other crimes. I'll keep your information in case anything new comes up. I do want to thank you for your help and concern in this case." With that he said good-bye and hung up.

What was going on? If that pizza guy had seen him and gotten the license number off Jared's car, then why the fuck didn't they haul his ass in? Jeff called Shawna at her work right away. "He doesn't think Jared has anything to do with these crimes. Said he doesn't fit the profile. Why do they keep blowing us off?"

"What about that eyewitness?"

"I don't know. I can't figure all this shit out. We know it's him… but they think it's somebody else."

"Jeff, Jared's gonna know it was us who reported him. No one else knows where he lives or anything about him. I thought they would arrest him on the spot."

"So did I. I can't believe this shit. We're gonna have to do this ourselves. Prove to them beyond any doubt that it's Jared who's doing all these murders. Let's follow him this Saturday again."

"We're gonna have to be extra careful that he doesn't see us. He'll probably have his guard up now. He knows we're on to him."

That Saturday, Shawna drove over to Jeff's so that she could spend the night when they got through with their detective duty. As soon as she arrived, Jeff guided her into the bathroom, "I'm gonna make you look like a man, if indeed that's possible. We're both gonna alter our appearances and I got a car from work again—a different one."

He had asked Shawna not to wear any make-up, so he went to work applying a mustache and beard that he had bought from a studio costume company. On went thicker eyebrows over the top of her own perfectly groomed ones. He again had her tuck her hair under a baseball cap.

He had also purchased a disguise for himself—a mustache and a wig with shaggy, shoulder length blond hair. He did not wear a cap. Didn't want to over do it—make them look like they were made up for a Halloween party or something.

They looked at each other with ominous seriousness this time. Neither saw any humor in their disguises or what they were about to undertake. Jeff had taken Duffy over to Kevin's condo for him to watch just in case Jared had found out where he lived. If Jared were to harm that little dog, he would administer the death penalty personally. They would pick Duffy up on their way home.

At two o'clock in the afternoon, they drove to North Hollywood and parked down the street where they would not be noticed but had a clear view of Jared's driveway. They had first driven by to make sure he was home. They sat and waited. They had come totally prepared this time with food, water and the infamous coffee can. Hours went by and there was no activity. They ate sandwiches and potato chips, which Shawna had brought from home and after three hours, both of them needed to use the facilities.

The shock of seeing Jared pull out into the street startled them into action. Again, Jeff hung back before pulling away from the curb. It was six o'clock and dark outside. A definite aid in their tailing endeavor.

Jared pulled onto the freeway headed towards Los Angeles. He did not exit for at least forty-five minutes. They followed him down an off ramp that emptied out onto a major boulevard. He drove some distance down this street, and then turned down a side street that led to a massive city park. It must have taken up at least twenty city blocks and it butted against the hills. Jeff looked over at Shawna. They both shook their heads in terrified anticipation.

"He's turning into a parking lot. I'm gonna drive on by, then turn around and come back."

When Jeff made a U turn at the next intersection, he killed the lights and slowly crept back down the street where Jared had parked in the lot. He parked on the street and they got out and carefully moved to the cover of a row of thick bushes. They watched as Jared took something out of his trunk. Something wrapped in a blanket.

He walked into the park. They followed. Jared kept on going deeper and deeper into a woodsy area. They had passed a playground, tennis courts and a large lake. He finally stopped at a group of picnic tables with gas barbeques placed at every other one. He sat down at one of the benches and laid the blanket on the tabletop. Jeff and Shawna had no trouble finding a hiding place, as the area was overgrown with trees and shrubs. They dove behind some thickly packed bushes and watched from where they had a bird's eye view.

Thirty minutes passed and Jared once again began to pace. He glanced down the path on which he had come and then paced to the opposite end of the benches where the path continued. He started pacing back and forth, obviously becoming more and more agitated—like a restless animal awaiting his prey.

All of a sudden, they heard footsteps. Someone was approaching. Jeff grabbed Shawna's hand and squeezed it tightly. What in God's name had they gotten themselves into?

A young girl emerged from the path and was walking toward the picnic area. Her blonde hair was brushing over her shoulders and she was wearing tight jeans and a heavy, winter jacket. She appeared hesitant, uncertain as to what she was walking into, but the instant she caught sight of Jared's dark silhouette, she stopped in her tracks. She froze for a few seconds as Jared lurked in the shadows—watching—waiting for his prey to come closer. All of a sudden, as if hit with the grim reality of the situation, she turned and started sprinting back up the pathway. He took off chasing her, but the adrenaline pumping through her body was giving her unanticipated speed. Jeff and Shawna ran after them, but Jared was too caught up in his wild fixation to notice them. He never looked back.

The girl ran at a full sprint back through the park—like a frightened jackrabbit being chased by a hungry mountain lion. Jared tailed her all the way to the parking lot where he almost caught her when she stood fumbling with her keys at her car door. She had barely slammed the door, when he caught up. He took a large bat from inside the blanket and began bashing it into her window. Completely immersed into his violent rampage, he would stop at nothing to get at her. He continued smashing the heavy object into the glass as she started up her car. The window was breaking away and he was able to slip his hands inside the car and grab a hold of her clothing. He pulled feverishly at her jacket, almost yanking her through the broken window. She shoved the car into reverse and backed out of the space, knocking Jared off his feet and onto the pavement. Then she peeled out at the speed of lightning, tires screeching loudly against the asphalt.

Jared jumped into his car and took off in pursuit. Jeff and Shawna ran across the street to their car and raced to catch up with Jared, but he had gotten too much of a head start and they lost him in the traffic of the boulevard. They pulled to the curb and Jeff grabbed his cell phone.

"911, what's your emergency?"

"We just witnessed the killer in an attempted murder in the park at Wilcox and State," Jeff shouted into his phone.

"Your name?"

"God-damn it! We just saw the serial killer laying in wait for his next victim! You gotta get the police out here fast. He's chasing a young girl down State Street. We were trying to follow them, but we lost him in traffic."

"I'm sorry sir, you'll have to calm down so that I can get your information. What is your location?"

"We just pulled out from the city park on Wilcox in Los Angeles."

"Couldn't this have been a simple lover's spat?"

"No, no! We know the young man who is doing these crimes. He's meeting his victims in city parks. You need to get the police on him right away. The poor girl's life is in imminent danger!"

"What is the make and license number of the suspect's vehicle?"

"It's a silver Honda Accord." He turned to Shawna. "What's the plate number?"

"I don't know," she answered, frantically trying to conjure up this information from her memory.

"We don't know the plate number," he reported, his voice shaking.

"And the make and plate number of the vehicle being pursued?"

"Well, I don't know. I didn't have a chance to get her license number. But the car looked like a black Ford Mustang."

"I'm ringing into the police station right now, sir. Do you know which way they headed?"

"They headed… wait a minute, let me think… south! They headed south on State. Please hurry."

"Okay, I'm giving your report to the police as we speak. They'll send the closest unit in the area to pursue the suspect." Jeff could hear her clicking rapidly on a computer keyboard. "Do you know the name and address of the girl being chased?"

"No," Jeff reported. "We saw her walk into the park. When she got a good look at Jared, she turned and made a swift beeline back to her car in the parking lot. He chased her and started beating the window in on the driver's side with a baseball bat."

The woman seemed startled by this last information. It was as if she had not taken Jeff's report seriously until she heard this. She immediately became intensely vigilant. "Sir, you say that you know this person?"

"Yes! Yes! It's my girlfriend's brother. No, no… I mean… it's her son." He could have kicked himself for this last blunder in speech. Now, he sounded like a complete buffoon.

"Sir, I've dispatched a patrol car in response to your report. Now, I see that I'm being trifled with. Do you realize the time and resources that are wasted when a call is fraudulent?"

"Oh, how can I make you understand? If you only knew the whole story. I can't explain it now. You just have to believe me."

But now, the operator was feeling the sting of being duped. Her patience was quickly wearing thin. The 911 service was plagued with bogus reports and prank calls like these were devastating to this crucial public assistance. She was now loosing her patience with this caller.

"Sir, please give me your name, address and telephone number."

Her one hundred and eighty degree turnaround in attitude was palpable. Feeling defeated, Jeff gave her the information she requested. She told him that she would contact him if there were any questions regarding this matter. She disconnected.

"What are we gonna do?" he threw up his hands to Shawna.

"Maybe we can call the police in the Valley and give the report to them. After all, they did come out to question him once. Maybe they'll believe us."

Jeff made the call going through the same annoying channels as before—being switched from this department to that department. Finally, he gave his report to someone—he did not know who. The man seemed very matter of fact. As if he were in no hurry to respond to Jeff's hysterical report.

With his eyes glazed over, he looked at Shawna. "Honey, I feel like we're in one of those horrible nightmares where you can't run and you can't scream and no one cares that you just witnessed a murder. It's like no one believes us! Don't they want to catch this serial killer?"

"I don't know, honey. Maybe they get so many prank calls and dead end leads that they just become complacent. Are they gonna stake out his house?"

"I don't know about staking out, but he said they'd check it out," Jeff reported as he pulled his fake mustache off and threw it, along with his wig, into the back seat. Shawna followed suit and set her disguise down as she scooted over into the protection of Jeffs arms.

All of a sudden her nerves turned to mush and she collapsed into a total emotional meltdown. "God, Jeff, I just watched Jared—the boy I knew since they first pulled him out of my body, try to murder another human being! I always knew he had his problems, but this… this…." Her sobs and shrieks of revulsion crashed through the fragile dam that had held them at bay. She became hysterical.

All Jeff could do was to hold her tightly as he, too, began to feel the hot sting of tears sliding down his face.

CHAPTER 34

After the two of them were able to grab a hold of their frazzled nerves, Jeff spoke softly, "Let's go drive by Jared's house and see if he's there. And honey, maybe you should hold off on going home—at least for a while. I don't want you alone." She simply nodded as she put her head on his lap.

They drove in silence back to Jared's house. When Jeff pulled up, there was not a cop car in sight. The house was dark. He pulled to the curb and called the police once again. After the predictable runaround, he finally got a woman detective who knew what she was talking about.

"We did send a squad car out there, but there was no activity—no one home. We can't just dispatch a car to sit there for hours but they will drive by at regular intervals until they are able to make contact. We have your name and phone number on file. We'll contact you as soon as we have any information to share with you. Sir, we very much appreciate your report and we intend to follow up to the fullest extent."

"Have the police in the precinct near State and Wilcox received a report from the girl we saw being chased through the park?" he queried.

"No sir, I'm checking that right now. No call was made regarding the assault that you witnessed. We'll keep you apprised."

Jeff thanked her and hung up. At least they seemed to believe him. He would make sure not to make such a blunder in speech again as he had done with the 911 operator. He really did get the feeling that this officer had taken him seriously and would stay on the case. His vision of having the entire police department drop everything to pursue Jared Reese was crumbling before his eyes. He had to realize that they had other things to do—other emergencies.

Still, he was feeling beaten. He felt as if he were in a deep nightmare from which he could not wake up—shaken to the very core of his being. Nothing of this night could possibly be real.

"They have been driving by," he reported to Shawna. "They haven't seen any activity yet. They'll keep on it till he comes home. Honey, are you up to going in and having a look around?"

"Yes." She smashed her hands into her face and broke down again. "My son is a murderer, Jeff! I gave birth to a serial killer! All from being raped and beaten and left for dead by his father! Those poor girls lost their lives in an unspeakable way all because of me!"

It wasn't her fault at all and he loved her with every fiber of his being. He tried desperately to console her by telling her that she had nothing to do with Jared's life choices. He was a completely separate soul from her. "He came through you—not from you," he told her. This seemed to calm her as she thought about it.

"Thank you, Jeff. I love you so much."

"I love you too, baby."

"You must! Who else would ever stick by me through all of this hell?"

He smiled. "Honey, if you're not up to going in, let's just forget it and go home."

"No. I'm definitely up to it. I want to see what's in there."

"Good thing we don't need a key," he said as he again pushed the door open.

"He hates calling anyone to do repairs—doesn't want strangers around—and he has no skills at all for fixing anything."

They stepped in with a profound feeling of trepidation lumped up in their throats.

"Mom, some teenagers attacked my car with baseball bats when I stopped at the intersection by the library," Pamela Maulhardt lied to her mother. She had to come up with some reason for the damage done to her mother's car. Her heart was still pounding wildly in her chest. "They came out of nowhere. I didn't even see them till they jumped all over the car. They started smashing my window with bats. I barely got out of there before they grabbed me through the broken window. Mom, I was so scared."

It would never due for her to tell her mother that she had met a boy in a chat room on line—and that that boy turned out to be the "Saturday Night Killer". She had promised her mother, faithfully, never to go to those sites.

She knew that she had just had a close brush with a serial killer—a close brush with a hideous death. But she could not tell of her experience in the park. She would be grounded forever and she just couldn't bear to see the disappointment in her mother's face at what an idiotic thing she had just done. So she made up the only lie that came to mind and her mother bought it.

"Oh honey, we need to call the police right away. Give them your report. Those boys were out to hurt somebody and you were at the wrong place at the wrong time," her mother exclaimed as she began dialing the phone.

"Mom, I so sorry about your car."

"Don't worry about the car, sweetheart. It wasn't your fault at all. I'll get it to the shop for a new window first thing in the morning. I'm just so relieved that you're all right. Oh, when I think of what might have happened," she cried as she gathered her daughter into her arms.

Pamela was forced to construct an elaborate lie when the officers came to take her statement. They seemed very calm—not particularly ruffled by her encounter. "Malicious mischief," they had called it. No connection was made between Jeff's 911 call and Pamela's broken window. She went to bed that night vowing never to disobey her parents again. She said a silent prayer of thanks to God for saving her life. Just why he had spared her and not the others, she did not know, but one thing for sure—she'd be a changed person from now on.

Jared had quickly abandoned his pursuit when he saw that his target was headed for home. For the first time, he was scared. Scared of getting caught. He had been so careless—leaving his DNA all over the place and probably a mass of other identifying clues. Now, he shook in terror that there was someone who had seen him plainly. Someone who could identify him. He had to think quickly. What to do? What to do?

But it was not only the events of this evening that had him distressed. Who except for his sister and that slime bucket boyfriend of hers could have called the police to come to his house to question him? He felt a surge of rage welling up from deep inside of him. How could they do that to him? What did they know of anything? "My sister doesn't even know who I am," he said aloud. "I've got to make her stop interfering in my life... once and for all."

CHAPTER 35

As soon as they stepped into the door, Jeff and Shawna could easily see that Jared had already been there. They searched each room of the house. "Looks like he went through here like a cyclone—grabbing everything he needed and what he thought might be incriminating—even his computer," Jeff said. "He's outta here. He'll never be back."

"I'm sure not," Shawna agreed. "He probably thinks that girl went right home to report the crime. Between her and us reporting him, he must be afraid to go home—or back to his job."

"No doubt about that," he agreed.

"But Jeff, he has a key to my apartment. He knows that I keep a large stash of money in a fake Pepsi can in the refrigerator. He'll probably go there and take the money. He has nothing else to survive on if he doesn't."

"Do you want to drive over there now? See if we can catch him?"

"You bet!"

"Got your gun?" he asked.

"Yup. Right here," she replied as she patted her purse.

He flashed her a curious look, "You know how to use that thing?"

"I'm not sure… God, I hope so. I took a class that was given by the police department, but that was years ago, now."

Jeff's face melted into an "are you shittin' me?" kind of look. She returned with a sheepish grin.

"Jesus, I hope we don't have to put it to the test."

With fear pulsating through every nerve in their bodies, they drove up and parked on the side street near Shawna's building. Both of her spaces in the carport were empty. They looked up and down the street, but did not spot Jared's Accord.

Shawna turned the key and pushed the door open. They walked into a dark apartment. She switched on the living room light, then went immediately to the refrigerator to check for her stash money. It was gone—Pepsi can and all.

"He's been here, too!" she shouted. "He took the money."

"It seems he's been a step ahead of us at every turn. How much was in there?"

"Two thousand dollars. I always kept cash just in case of an earthquake or some other emergency."

"Good idea. I do the same thing. But I wonder how long he can exist on two thousand dollars. He'll need food and gas—and a place to stay."

She shook her head. "I don't know if he'll get some broken down hotel room or if he'll just sleep in his car. If he thinks it through at all, he'll know that he's a sitting duck in that car. He'll probably think that both he and his car have been identified and that we must have given the police the plate number."

"I'm sure you're right. But the only person who asked for his plate number was that 911 operator and I'm fairly sure I know where that report ended up."

"We didn't give it to her anyway. I don't even know where to look for information on that car. It must be packed away somewhere. Maybe in one of those boxes in your garage. They'd have to run a DMV search to get it."

"What about that pizza guy who saw him at the scene a couple of weeks ago?" Jeff said. "They said he got the plate number. There's something I'm just not getting here."

"Me either. Something's terribly wrong."

They searched the apartment thoroughly but did not notice anything else missing. Shawna had her diamond earrings stashed safely in her purse.

"Well, let's go pick up Duffy then head back to my house."

"You two look like death warmed over," Kevin said as he stood to the side to let them through the doorway. "What's going on?"

Jeff picked up Duffy who was squealing and jumping all over his legs. Kevin gestured for them to sit and they filled him in on all of the insane events of the night. Kevin was riveted for this was the most intriguing and exhilarating real life event he had ever been part of.

"What are you gonna do now?" he asked.

"We haven't really sat down to devise a plan yet. We're pretty sure he doesn't know where I live so I think we're safe there for tonight."

Shawna looked as if she were deep in thought. "You know what I think? When he runs out of money, he'll come back to my apartment. I mean, how long can a person live on two thousand dollars? He'll hit me up for money and food—I just know it."

"Maybe you two should stay at Shawna's to lay in wait for him. Since the police aren't gonna stake the place out, you'll have a much better chance of catching him there," Kevin offered.

"Are you tryin' to get us killed?" Jeff bristled.

"No man, I'm tryin' to help catch him. I'll stay there if you want…as long as you give me the gun."

"Are you crazy? Who do you think you are—Clint Eastwood?"

Kevin shook his head. "What's your suggestion Mr. Sherlock Holms?"

"Well, we know he's not only dangerous—he's a goddamned serial killer!" But as quickly as the words escaped his mouth, he knew how much this must have hurt Shawna. Had she not been through enough agony already? He looked over to see tears welling in her eyes. "I didn't mean for that to come out sounding so callous, honey. I just get carried away when I talk to Kevin. We never pull any punches with each other."

"It's okay. I don't want you to be careful around me. I know what Jared is. I have to face it… head on."

After talking into the night, they did formulate a plan of action. Jeff would stay with Shawna at her apartment. They would come there after work on Monday and spend every day and night until Jared came back. Also, Jeff decided to hire a private investigator to watch the apartment during the day when they both would be away at work. He would instruct the investigator to follow Jared. That way they could send the police to the place where he was holed up to apprehend him.

Kevin would stay at Jeff's house (an opportunity on which he always leaped) and baby-sit Duffy. He offered to help with anything they needed—even if it were dangerous, he didn't care.

They took Duffy home and spent the rest of the weekend at the house. Kevin would move in on Monday to start his babysitting assignment.

CHAPTER 36

Twelve squad cars surrounded the trailer of a William James Bucklin where he had resided by himself for the past year and a half. Neighbors had reported suspicious goings on several times, but after brief interviews, the police would inevitably leave empty handed. Mr. Bucklin would be observed taking young girls into his trailer, however; no one was able to identify any of these girls as victims of the recent serial killer. "It was just too damned dark," the elderly woman across the way reported. "But, I heard things—things like a man and a woman arguing and screams sometimes."

The police were called out more than once, but each time they came, he was already gone with the young lady or he was home and welcomed the officers in. There would never be anyone there with him and he was always ready with a story that he and his girlfriend had had words, then she stormed out and went home. They would look around each time, however; after finding nothing incriminating, they left.

Their big break was when the pizza deliveryman who, through quick thinking, had nabbed the plate number on Bucklins' 96' Chevy truck. The vehicle was registered to him at an old address, but they eventually tracked him here to where he now resided in an old, rundown trailer. This, along with additional evidence they had gathered would, at last, bring the recent string of homicides to an end.

The trailer park was, for the most part, occupied by elderly, disabled or derelict type people—many of whom had little to occupy themselves but to keep an eagle eye on what their neighbors were up to. "Good for them!" Officer Tannack told his rookie partner. "It was because of them that our suspicions were piqued to begin with. Then, when we were able to trace his truck to this address, we knew we had our man."

It was an exciting night at the "Shady Acre's Trailer Park" as every single resident watched William Bucklin being escorted out of his home in handcuffs. He was a very ordinary looking man of about forty years of age. His demeanor was actually friendly as he walked past his neighbors—nodding to each one in a pleasant greeting. He slid into the patrol car without an argument.

A team of forensic specialists was already swarming the place in an effort to gather every bit of evidence they could find. At last, they could go over the entire residence with a fine-tooth comb.

Deluges of questions were being fired at the officers, "Is he the Saturday Night Killer?" "Is this the man who killed all those girls?" "Are you gonna give him the chair?" The officers answered with non-committal responses, "We are not at liberty to answer any questions at this time." "Please go back into your homes, everything is being taken care of."

The suspect was driven to the Van Nuys division and later booked on suspicion of first-degree murder. They had him. In the next few days he would appear in a line up so that the eyewitness could identify him, and then his mouth would be swabbed and the specimen sent out for DNA testing—the final link they needed to formally charge him and set a date for trial.

CHAPTER 37

It was a small, dingy motel room, but it was a safe hideaway for the time being. And if Jared had to be honest, it was quite a bit more comfortable than his bungalow. The heat worked in here, which was a dramatic improvement over his old place. The furnace had quit on him shortly after he moved in, but he had an aversion to calling the landlord to make the necessary repairs. He decided he'd rather put up with the cold than have people traipsing in and out of his private space. And here, he had a queen-sized bed with clean sheets and a warm blanket and comforter under which to slide for a good night's sleep. And that was all he wanted to do after this night of complete fiasco.

He awakened late the next morning, planning his next move and his strategy for the upcoming weeks. "I know I gotta get outta here thanks to that fucking girl and my sister. Between the two of them, they've probably got the cops hot on my trail."

He decided that he would move east—maybe to New York or some other place on the east coast. They would never know anything about him there. He could start all over again. But, it would take money to get that far—even driving. Then, he would need to rent an apartment. He would need a great deal of money for that. Shawn owed him enough to get him started in his new life. What the fuck—she had plenty of money. He knew she had at least fifteen thousand in her savings—and the sale of their mom's house. That should've brought another fifty thousand, easy. And half of that was supposed to be his. Mom had left it to both of them—not just Shawna. That greedy bitch had swindled him!

She had no doubt replaced the stash money in the refrigerator by now. And she had some valuable jewelry—diamond necklaces and those earrings her piece 'o shit boyfriend gave her. He still had most of the two thousand he had lifted from her apartment. That along with whatever the jewelry sold for would give him plenty of cash to get settled in a new place.

But first, he hungered for one more girl. His last attempt having been thwarted, he ached for the soft, warm flesh of one more victim before he headed east. "I'll lay low for a while—just hangin' out here, then I'll go hunting."

Unable to hook up his computer, Jared felt agitated at his present situation. There had been, at least, six girls that were eager to meet with him, but now he had no possible way of making a connection with any of them, so he would have to look for a nice, young female through some other method. After deep thought and consideration, he decided to cruise through the section of town that hosted the seedy side of humanity—the "willing to do anything for bucks" girls that staked their claims along the dark end of Sepulveda Boulevard.

Driving slowly along this district, he spotted a number of available females. Ones that probably no one cared much about. Ones that would most likely go unnoticed for quite some time. One last taste of yielding flesh and he would be on to greener pastures—all except for one last task, that is.

He pulled up alongside a fairly attractive blond. Hard looking though—not like the soft young things he was used to. Rolling the window down, he asked her to get in. To his surprise, she leaned into the open window and told him her price, "A hundred dollars for intercourse—and fifty more for the room. I supply the room."

Her forceful demeanor took him aback, but he went along with her demands. He fumbled around in his pocket for a time, then produced two, one hundred dollar bills. Her eyes widened and she instructed him to park on the side street around the corner.

When he came walking up to her, she recoiled at the sight of him, but waved him forward to follow her. He trailed her into a grimy looking motel where she stopped at a downstairs door and opened it with a key that she had pulled out of her pocket. He followed her in. She closed and locked the door behind him, then she sat down on top of the double bed.

"The money first," she demanded, snapping her fingers at him.

"Okay," he said as he handed her the two, crisp hundred-dollar bills.

She took them and placed them in a small purse that she had carried in. She laid it down on the bedside stand and proceeded to remove her clothing.

Seeing her close up like this, she did not look attractive at all. In fact, she looked old… dumpy. Her ugliness along with her abrupt manner was stirring up even more violence on Jared's insides. He quickly decided that he hated this bitch—loathed her.

She spread her legs and motioned for him to climb on top of her. He pulled off his pants and briefs and threw them on the floor. He mounted her and started pumping away as hard as he could. She was different from the others—not as tight, not as soft, but it felt okay. A different kind of excitement. He had never had a girl who was willing—paid for or not.

After he exploded into her, he looked closely at her face. She did not look back at him, but held her face to the side—waiting for him to get off of her. When he did not, she gave him an impatient shove. Without a thought, he grabbed the telephone that was sitting on the bedside stand and smashed it down onto her forehead. He smashed it and smashed it until blood started spraying out in all directions, then his hands went around her thin neck and he began to squeeze.

Her eyes met his with horror and he squeezed harder—much harder. She struggled to free herself, but she was no match for Jared's crushing grip. He watched as the life drained from her face—from her body. It pleased him very much to snuff the life's breath out of this whore.

He lay on top of her for a while, then got up and took his money back out of her purse—along with another seventy-five dollars that was already in there. He peeled his shirt off and stuffed it under his arm. When he exited the room, no one was around. He was sure no one had caught sight of him.

As he walked up to his car, he noticed an old, disabled Ford Pinto up on blocks in someone's driveway up the street a ways. He grabbed some tools from his trunk and removed the license plates from the vehicle, then he exchanged these plates with the ones on his own car. *No one's gonna notice the plates on this old car,* he thought.

No sooner had he closed the door of his car to start his journey back to his motel room, than his body wrenched at the sight of a patrol car cruising slowly past him with its lights off. He stared at the officer and their eyes met. Jared quickly looked away and started up the engine of his Accord. The police car continued past him and made a U turn at the end of the short, dead-end street.

When it came up along side him, it stopped. The officer glared at Jared for a few seconds, then moved on. He made a left turn at the corner. Jared had never been so terrified in his life. Trembling, he pulled out and made a right turn at the same corner. He pulled down an alley a safe distance from the motel and put the car in park. He removed his pants, then wadded them up with his bloody shirt and tossed them into someone's garbage bin. After quickly slipping into the clean shirt and pants he had brought along, he drove cautiously back to his room.

He jumped into the shower to wash off the blood that had spattered all over his skin, then he dropped onto the bed and vowed not to go out again until he was to leave town. That was, except for one last stop.

CHAPTER 38

Weeks passed and no sign of Jared. If only they had some clue where he would have gone to hide out, if indeed, he was even in the area anymore. But things were actually getting back to some semblance of normalcy as Shawna had brought home the makings for her famous spaghetti sauce. It was a Saturday night and she wanted to make a special meal for Jeff. She bought a very expensive bottle of wine and a drop dead, to die for yummy, strawberry and whipped cream cake that she purchased from her favorite bakery.

"That was the most incredible meal I've ever eaten," Jeff raved.

After he helped with the dishes, he offered his hand and they danced from one end of the apartment to the other—just like when they first met. He waltzed her around, twirling her and dipping her. They were both giddy with laughter. Letting go completely, they had more genuine fun than they had had in months. When they tired of waltzing, they cuddled up on the sofa and listened to music for a while, then they went to bed and made love—passionate, thrilling, liberating love. Although the thought of Jared "out there somewhere" was indeed troubling, they could finally relax and fully indulge in their love that was growing more intense by the day. Capping off such an incredible evening, they fell asleep in each other's embrace.

At 2:10 AM, Shawna's keen ear heard a suspicious noise. It

took only seconds to identify the sound—a key in the lock. She instantly started shaking her sound asleep boyfriend.

"Honey," she whispered. "He's here. I hear him unlocking the door."

"Oh shit," he barked, trying to shake the cobwebs out of his head.

He grabbed the phone and quickly dialed 911, but before it was answered a large hand came down hard on his, slamming the receiver back down onto its cradle. He looked up to see a massive figure posed in the shadows above the bed.

The weeks without a sign of him had caused them to become a bit complacent—not having a chance to prepare themselves for this altercation. Where was that gun? Where the hell was it? A little too much wine was clouding their otherwise sharp minds.

The hand came down again—this time wielding a heavy meat cleaver. Jeff rolled to the side of the bed just in time to miss the plunging blow. Shawna was on her feet racing to locate her purse… and the gun which was sitting somewhere on the bottom of it.

What to do… what to do? Oh God, quick!

"Jared!" Jeff shouted. "We wanna help you, for Christ's sake!" But the cleaver slammed down again. In a blow that was aiming for his skull, Jeff instantly turned away and the ax came down hard, missing his head, but piercing deeply into his shoulder muscle—stopped only by his clavicle bone. He howled in agony.

Shawna was frantically rummaging through her humongous purse in search of their only hope for survival. She felt a heavy thud followed by the sharp sting of unbearable pain sinking deeply into the flesh of her back. No sooner had she turned towards her attacker and she felt it again—this time more than she could bear.

He's killing Shawna! Jeff thought as he pulled his injured body across the room to where Jared continued hacking at his sister. Throbbing in pain, Jeff crept up behind him. Grabbing his long, stingy hair, he slammed his fist into Jared's neck with all of the strength he could muster. Instantly Jared swirled around to deliver another sinking blow from the heavy ax. A blow that plunged into Jeff's chest—ripping through his muscles. He could hear the hideous sound of his own rib bones splintering.

This injury rendered him unable to raise his right arm so all he could do was watch as Jared elevated his weapon once again. All of a sudden the world stopped. It was as if everything was moving in slow motion. There was nothing Jeff could do to save himself. Thoughts of Duffy, his family, his work, Kevin and finally Shawna raced through his mind. He would never have a life with the only woman he had ever really loved. He would never again hold her in his arms. Never again see any of his loved ones. This was it. His life was ending at the hands of his lover's child.

A crash like thunder reverberated through his ears, shaking his whole body down to the core of his being. The earth shuttered, as he lay there unable to move—fighting to stop the wild spinning inside his head. Then he heard the blast twice more as something ripped through the air above his head at the speed of lightning.

After a few seconds, he rolled over and saw his attacker lying on the bedroom floor three feet in front of him, his body contorted. He was motionless... blood seeping from his chest like fast moving rivers, the meat cleaver still clutched tightly in his right hand.

Shawna was on him in one swift movement to make sure that he would not lash out on them again though she was bleeding badly from her injuries.

"You turned me in. You ratted out your own flesh and blood—your own brother," he forced the words out.

"Not my brother," she told him. "My son. You are my son, Jared."

His eyes became enormous with astonishment. "You're... my mother?"

"Yes. You were the product of a rape and attempted murder on me. Your father was a serial killer in Oregon. You were the result of his twenty some odd murder attempt. Mom and Dad raised you with so much love, and I did too, but you pushed our love away at every turn."

She held his head as tears started running down his face and for the first time in his life, Shawna saw something behind those eyes. A faint spark of remorse perhaps—as if a deep understanding of what he had done was at last piercing through the heavy walls that caged his soul.

"I'm sorry, Shawn. I don't know what's wrong with me. I always knew something was terribly, terribly wrong—but I can't stop. I try so hard to push down the evil thoughts and fantasies, but they just keep popping right back up—getting stronger all the time." He began to cry. Sobs that finally came bubbling up to the surface. A lifetime of sin was purging from the very hub of his being. "I don't want to do these things, but something inside keeps driving me. This urge to kill takes over my every thought. I'm afraid of my own mind!" he screamed in agony. "If you only knew what all I've done. I'm an evil monster!"

"No, you're not…but you behave as one." she cried. "Jared, did you kill Dad? I've wondered about it all this time. Even back then, I thought, maybe you did it. That you pushed my darling father off our roof… did you?"

"I had to kill him, Shawna. He found all my stuff and he said he was gonna turn me in. I knew I had to do something before he had me committed. He said he was gonna take care of me as soon as the heavy rains stopped. Said he was ashamed of me. That I was not really his son." He stopped and mulled this over. "Now I know what he meant. I really wasn't his son."

"Oh Jared, Dad and all those innocent young girls."

"Dad and all those girls," he echoed. "I can see their faces now, Shawna. They're coming closer!" She watched as his eyes filled with horror. He was looking beyond her, beholding something that was far too terrifying for words. His mouth opened to scream, but no sound came out. His body convulsed—then his head dropped to the side.

Jeff crawled over to her and took her into his arms as best he could with one arm disabled. "Are you all right?" he managed to speak. She nodded as she nestled into him and they lay on the bedroom floor in each other's embrace—both still bleeding profusely from their hatchet wounds.

In no time at all, the apartment was filled with paramedics and police officers. 911 had received numerous reports of gunshots and screams coming from apartment 11.

Shock and loss of blood overcame the two of them and they felt themselves passing out—unable to keep a hold of consciousness. The evilness of the night faded into the shadows and a strange calm fell upon them… then nothingness.

Both Jeff and Shawna awakened in hospital beds—each asking for the other. Each feeling the agonizing reminder that the horrific nightmare had actually taken place. Large doses of morphine helped little to dull their pain. The razor-sharp burn of their wounds still cut through like a knife. "May I have something for the pain?" Shawna begged the nurse who was attending her dressings.

"We have you on a morphine drip, but I can give you a shot every four hours. Would you like one now?"

"Please," she said as unconsciousness again overcame her.

Jeff opened his eyes to see his parents, brothers, sisters and Kevin standing over his bed. "Did you check on Shawna?" he moaned.

"We've been back and forth between your rooms for the past three days," his father, Ray, reassured him. "She's just down the hall, son. She's gonna be fine… and so are you. The doctor said both of you will make a full recovery. Thank God."

"Is Jared…?"

"He's dead," Kevin told him. "Shawna shot him three times. He died at the scene."

"So, it's over?"

"All over, buddy."

CHAPTER 39

The next week, although still in agony every time he moved, Jeff was feeling a great deal better. He and Shawna were now being walked very slowly down the hall to each other's rooms by the orderly. They would sit and visit with one another for at least an hour, then the orderly would come and walk them back to their beds. This was truly the highlight of their day.

Each day, the nurse came in to take a "peek" under Jeff's dressings. He found this most amusing. Why didn't they just peel the bandages off and look at his friggin' hatchet gashes? But no—she always approached him in the most gingerly manner saying, "I'm just gonna take a little peek at your wounds." Then she would pry the bandages cautiously from the corners and peer under without lifting the dressing too much. He had to stifle a gut laugh at these times. Actually, it hurt like hell to laugh—so he gave the nurse a great big grin instead.

Also, his appetite was returning with a vengeance. This morning, he licked his lips in eager anticipation of the aromatic breakfast that was being brought in by the aide. Scrambled eggs, hash browns, applesauce, tomato juice, and coffee with cream— he could hardly wait to devour every morsel.

She slid his bed table so that it was easily reachable, then she removed his tray from the cart. But just as she was about to set it down in front of him, she slipped on something wet on the floor and her feet went right out from under her. Without a thought, she grabbed onto Jeff's table and dumped the entire tray of food and drink all over the front of him.

He lay there drenched in a sea of dripping, sticky food. Catching her mortified gaze, he stated matter-of-factly, "Well, looks like things are back to normal."

The girl pushed the call button then began frantically working to brush the food off of him. An orderly brought new linens and a fresh gown. She heard Jeff chuckling.

"I'm glad you're finding something funny in this situation. I would have thought you'd be furious with me."

"After what I've just been through, nothing could ever be that serious again."

In the weeks that followed, Jeff and Shawna were both released from the hospital. Jared's bungalow, the motel room and Shawna's apartment were all taped off as "crime scenes." The two were staying at Jeff's house and his mother and sisters took turns checking in on them and bringing food—lots and lots of food. Kevin and Cassie also visited daily bringing even more food—mostly take out from Pedro's. This was always a treat for Jeff, not only because it was his favorite restaurant, but because it made things seem so normal again.

Jeff's sister, Betsy, went out and purchased toiletries, pajamas, a robe, slippers, underwear, walking shoes and some comfortable sweat outfits for Shawna. She knew it would be a long time before they were able to retrieve anything from her apartment. Shawna was beside herself with appreciation. Everyone was being so generous and helpful. The two of them were deeply comforted by the love of friends and family—and most of all each other.

DNA results showed that Jared was indeed the "Saturday Night Killer." The one who was sexually assaulting his victims. He had been meeting teenaged girls in chat rooms. He would present himself as the seventeen-year-old son of wealthy parents and somehow, knowing the right things to say, he would lure his prey to city parks where he would beat them senseless, rape them, murder them, then either dump their bodies at other locations or just leave them where they were. Now, Shawna knew why his clothing kept disappearing—they must have become soaked in blood and he was forced to discard them. Law enforcement also matched Jared's DNA with several bodies up in Oregon. It appeared that he had started his murdering spree a few years ago.

William James Bucklin was also the "Saturday Night Killer." The one who did not sexually violate his victims. The two perpetrators' patterns being almost identical, the police had thought that one man was responsible for all of the recent killings. That there were two men out there hunting did not even occur to them. In the subsequent months, Bucklin was tried and convicted, by a jury of his peers, to life in prison without possibility of parole. After the conviction, he confessed to all of the murders he had committed. The two serial killers were out of commission for good.

The police had impounded the silver Honda Accord where they found bloodstains, blanket fibers and a wealth of other evidence. The body of the prostitute was quickly identified as one of Jared's victims.

The motel room, in North Hollywood, where he had been holed up for the last few weeks of his life was also closed off until all of the evidence could be gathered. There, they had found his porno, his bats, his computer and several pieces of jewelry that he had lifted off the bodies of his victims. Th pieces were identified by family members of the de girls. The headline read: Jared Michael Reese, son of convicted serial killer, Ivan Lee Adler and William James Bucklin, loner, although completely unknown to one another, will forever share the brand of "Saturday Night Killer."

"I can't believe I killed my own son." Shawna said despondently as she, Jeff and Duffy sat out on his terrace enjoying the evening.

"He gave you no choice. He was going to kill us. You saved my life that night."

"Only after you saved mine," she reminded him.

"And you probably saved the lives of dozens of young, innocent girls. He had no intention of giving up his career in murder."

"Thanks, Jeff. I needed to hear that. I needed to know there was no other way than what I did. It's a heavy thing—killing somebody. I know I'll never be the same for the rest of my life. How could he do that to people and actually take pleasure in it?"

"Only a very sick mind would do something like that," Jeff consoled. "None of this was your fault at all. I don't ever want to hear you blame yourself for one thing that happened. You and your parents gave him all of the love and help you possibly could. It was entirely his choice to live the life he did."

"You're right. We only wanted to love him. He just wouldn't let us." Just then a far away look came across her eyes. "But now I have no one. No family at all."

"You can have mine," he offered.

"Oh Jeff, you shouldn't make jokes like that. Surely you don't want to get rid of them. You have such a wonderful family."

"I'm not trying to get rid of them. I'm asking you to become a part of us—will you marry me?"

She glanced up to see the adoring look in his eyes. "You want to marry me after all I've put you through?"

"Honey, you have suffered more agony than any human should ever have had to endure. I don't know how you have one ounce of sanity left. I admire and adore you with all my heart and soul. There's nothing that would make this man happier than if you would share your life with me forever… but a peaceful one, please," he teased as he raised his hand up in protest.

"Yes! Yes! Yes!" she shouted with delight. She leaned into him as their lips blended into a long, rapturous kiss.

"I just have one little thing that I have to ask," Jeff said after they parted their embrace.

"What's that?"

"You don't want to have children, do you?"

She reached up and turned his face to look him square in the eye, "HELL NO!!!"

Made in the USA
Columbia, SC
14 May 2024